GW00703044

THE
CRAB MAN

A Novel

by

Claire Wilkinson

Pen Press Publishers Ltd

Copyright Claire Wilkinson 2006

All rights reserved.
No part of this publication may be reproduced, stored in or introduced into a retrieval system, or transmitted, in any form,
or by any means (electronic, mechanical, photocopying,
recording or otherwise) without the prior written
permission of the publisher.

The characters in this book are fictional with the exception of Baba.
Any similarities to real people is entirely coincidental.

ISBN10: 1-905621-10-8
ISBN13: 978-1-905621-10-1

First published in Great Britain in 2006 by

Indepenpress Publishing
Pen Press Publishers Ltd
39 Chesham Road
Brighton
East Sussex BN2 1NB

A catalogue record for this book is available from
the British Library

Printed and bound in England

Cover design by Jacqueline Abromeit

I am ever present to those
who have realised me in every creature.
Bhagavad Gita

Heartfelt thanks to the following
for their assistance and huge encouragement

Joanna Levingston, Ann Shaw, Ani Whitely, Adrian and
Sue Whyte, Viv and John Packer, Miranda Ravetto Wood,
Agata Amala, Chris Knight, Andrew Carchrae, Amanda
Mellotte, Kees Van Dam, Avis Llewallan, June Watts, my
children and grandchildren and all those who have helped
in the production of The Crab Man and lastly my mentor,
John Sherlock – without whom this book would never
have been started.

To all those fabulous women whose quiet courage and strength are my inspiration.

NEW YORK 1991

Chapter 1

The violence with which I slammed the porch door shakes the walls and leaves them trembling. Tiny pieces of plaster dislodge themselves and float, like dust caught in sunlight, onto the tiled hall floor. Under my bare feet I feel the barest tremor as the foundations of the house stir with the unaccustomed force. "It's over!" I scream. Again. And again. And again. Every atom of my strained being, every stretched nerve, every last ounce of energy contained within that alien sound that leaves my body and hangs in the loaded air. And in that one moment it is. Over, I mean. Not just my second brief sham of a marriage but my whole life, it seems. A split second is all it takes. My foundations stirred so deeply that they could never settle back into complacency again. As if one of those cheese wire cutters, that slice so precisely, has just severed that portion of my life up until now and got rid of it.

As the noise from the crashing door fades, I hear my husband's retreating footsteps receding, like my life, which I watch slide away across the marble cheese slab, to be wrapped and hidden in the dark corner of someone else's basket. To be taken away. Gone. Disappeared forever. The volcano has finally erupted and nothing can stop it now. The simmering pot has blown its lid after what seems like a forever of trying to hold down that bubble that arises so often in my head. The trapped cobra, writhing and seething inside an earthenware jar of smooth and polished exterior.

Immersed in that endless mechanical existence, I would go through the monotonous daily routine. Rise at 6am. Put the cat out. Put the kettle on. Brush my teeth. Take a shower. Get dressed. Pour a coffee. Drink coffee. Let cat in. Feed cat. Look in kitchen cupboards to see if I need to buy more coffee, washing powder or toilet paper. Grab the car keys. Shout to boring husband ("Bye honey!") – still snoring – and leave for the florist's shop. *My* florist's shop. It isn't much – just one of those tiny glass conservatories you see on the sidewalk on so many street corners in the city. But it is all mine. Why, I even have an assistant, Jeannie. My old high school friend. By 8am the fresh flowers have been bought from the display in the wholesale travelling truck. That earthy evocative smell of damp wood, moss, dew and mingled heady perfumes as the double doors are opened to reveal their exotic contents. A jungle of colour that never fails to arouse my senses for a few seconds each day and transport me to a place of unclear yearning.

Now as I watch my husband hesitate then turn on the steps, I know the cobra is gloriously free. That smooth and polished exterior can never be put together again. The leash has snapped. The wild horse has taken the bit. At 6pm on a hot August evening in Brooklyn, New York, I, Chloe Fairchild, forty-eight-year-old wife, wage-earner and mother, just became my own person.

Euphoria and something unidentifiable coursing through me propels me into the dark kitchen, where I pour myself a large glass of chilled Chardonnay. Emptying the fridge of milk and carrying the three cartons into the bathroom, tipping them into the tub and turning the taps full on. While it is filling, plugging Andrea Bocelli into the socket outside the door so that we can sing along together as Cleopatra soaks in her organic, unpasteurised and unpolluted goat's milk bath. Before I get into the steaming water, rummaging in the back of the closet and finding that trailing Isadora Duncan scarf in the hideous yellow that Brett had so hated, and winding it around my long curly hair. En route back to the bathroom, slowly dropping my clothes one by one and leaving them lying where they fall, viewing with distaste the greying bra and dull knickers. The debris of a dull life just past. Tomorrow, I will replace them with something far sexier. Lacy maybe. Desirable even!

That desirable thought sends an unexpected quiver down my spine. How long since I felt desirable? On passing the kitchen, pouring another glass of wine, which seems to have gone down so fast. On second thoughts, as I am planning to spend some time luxuriating, I pour another and take the two, place them on the little stencilled table, pull it close to the tub. A captured glance in the long mirror isn't such a great idea. I will have to ring the gym tomorrow and enquire about aerobics classes and maybe some highlights to hide the grey, and perhaps a facial? Remembering that young taut body, those small but cheeky breasts, the perfectly rounded buttocks and comparing the slipped reality, I feel the briefest split second of something like depression but, on taking another sip and turning up the sultry voice of Andreas, it passes almost before I recognise it.

With the yellow scarf wound around her hair, a turbaned Cleopatra climbs into her milky pool, lies back and views her life ahead. Before me lies uncharted territory stretching far into the horizon. As Andreas' voice soars along with mine, I open my arms wide to embrace my new life. The dramatic sweeping gesture knocks my glass from the table at the same moment as the telephone rings. "Shit!"

"Mom, are you all right?" It is the anxious voice of my daughter Rosie.

"Never been better," I reply, perhaps a shade too brightly.

"Only Brett just phoned. Says you've been acting kind of strange lately. He sounds upset. Mom, he's worried about you."

"You bet he is," I mutter savagely under my breath, imagining Brett in the call booth on the corner with that assumed bewildered look on his face. "Sweetheart, great to talk to you but I'm dripping all over the floor, stark naked and beginning to shiver, and I don't have time right now to talk as I have a whole life ahead of me and such a lot of planning to do. Bye honey." I cut her off before she can reply, then drink another glass of wine, add more hot water to the tub, climb back in and close my eyes. Freedom, choices, stretching as far as I can see.

The crying begins at 23.01 precisely. I know that because Tabitha, my faithful old black and white cat, jumps on the counterpane and wakes me. The luminous hands on the fluorescent pink perspex clock so beloved by Brett tell me the time. As she tenderly curls into the small of my back and softly purrs, the floodgates open. I pull the sheet up over my head, curl into a ball and in that gentle darkness retreat back into the womb and howl. And from that safe place begins the mourning for my lost life, the sheet I lie on drenched with my tears that just flow on and on. With each tear a little bit of pain loosens and releases its hold. I watch it go.

At noon the next day Rosie's shaken face appears above the pulled-back sheet and invades my wet refuge.

"Mom, what are you doing?" Her voice is shaking. "Shall I call Doctor Brady?"

"Go away, Rosie, I'm perfectly fine."

"I've never seen you like this before, Mom." Fear makes her sound angry.

"I have every intention of crying as much and for as long as I wish to, so please go away and leave me alone." And with that I dive back into the womb and continue my watery but very necessary journey, Rosie's furious voice hardly penetrating as she tells me to pull myself together. Brett has been trying to call, she says. The cat has scratched the paint on the back of the front door trying to get out and then peed on the carpet.

"I'm going to ring Marjorie," she hisses before banging out of the room. Marjorie is my sister. Sometime later I hear a muffled sound like the door slamming again.

Over the next two weeks I rarely move out of the house but divide my time between bed and the bathroom. Taking numerous baths and sipping numerous glasses of wine and crying into the tub water. Sad music wafts through the house and if I have to go out for cigarettes, dark glasses are *de rigueur*. My eyelids, so swollen I barely recognise myself, and a diet of black coffee and cigarettes causing the weight to drop off me. At least once a day Rosie calls by but rarely stays longer than a few minutes. Brett rings, and Marjorie from LA. *How many more times do I have to tell them that I am really all right?* I wonder wearily. It is going to take more than a few days to rediscover myself. And with that thought comes the terror. The overwhelming fear. What if I never find myself again? Who am I really? Have I ever known? Perhaps I'm just a middle-aged woman having a breakdown? And, worst of all, perhaps there is nothing more to life than what I have known. Fear holds me in her teeth now, just as the relief, the euphoria, the pain and the crying has.

If you had asked my attorney father, a true traditionalist from a long line of traditionalists, to whom appearances were so very important, he would have taken on a pained expression and told you in that disapproving tone that I was 'headstrong'. That I had a bad track record. "Just like Great Aunt Lil," he would state in exasperation. I never knew Great Aunt Lil but I sure did like the sound of the old girl. Eccentric, warm-hearted and hopeless with money and men. Or so it seemed to my father. She never married but chose instead to take a string of lovers. Daring lady. Mostly oriental! *Tut tut!* More disapproving sounds. "And squandered her money by giving it away!" more tuts and more disapproval. "But at least she lived," I had attempted to say not so long ago. At this my father's temper, which was as large as his fortune – and his fortune had been considerable – appeared to be engaged in some kind of struggle as his cheeks grew purple and his eyes smaller and blacker. His lips pursed in readiness, his chest swelled and I was cut down to size. Felled. A few words were all it had ever taken.

"That, if I may say so, is an extremely ignorant remark!" This he said loudly, with the emphasis on the 'ignorant'. "Great Aunt Lil let down the family name and reputation." *What name? And who cares?* I dared to think but never uttered. The force with which these barbs had been delivered over the years made any attempt at arguing out of the question. Better to retreat into the cage, curl down crushed into the jar and give him the satisfaction of thinking all was in order again. The cage door firmly shut, the lid tightly on the jar, the cobra under control. *His* control. Damn him! That smooth, polished and (dare I even think it?) shallow exterior was all that counted. Nothing else. Standards had to be upheld. This was the recurrent theme threaded throughout my childhood: woven into the fabric of my formative years this belief that the real me, if allowed to escape, would bring into disgrace the family name and my father's reputation as a powerful and well-known attorney.

But who is the real me? I can't seem to remember.

The truth of the matter was that I was a disappointment. I wasn't the son this ambitious man thought he needed to follow his traditional theme. For my elder sister, Marjorie, it had been different. When she was born one bright November day, there was still some hope but after my difficult birth my mother was advised to have no more children. I don't think he ever forgave her.

Six months ago my father died, as he had lived: in control, until the last few hours. As I sat with my mother by his bedside he finally relinquished the reins and set me free.

Can the neglected spirit shed the straitjacket? Is it too

late for this woman I now saw in the mirror? The passionate young woman who had tried so hard to curb the wildness? Strained so hard *not* to be like Great Aunt Lil (who I so secretly admired and longed to emulate), so that my father could be proud of me? Curling into a tight ball, my arms crossed behind my back the silent scream rips through me. "*Help me find me!*" The unleashed cobra spinning around and around in circles of frightening bewilderment. The cage door is finally open, the lid off the pot, but what now? I am at a complete loss. Unbridled, running free, but I don't know where to bolt. At the end of the second week Jeannie appears for the second time. The first time, a week ago, she had simply taken one look at me and held out her arms. I was off again. As the tears cascaded it wasn't difficult to believe that our bodies are made up mostly of water!

But this time I am ready to get away. Somewhere where I have the necessary solitude to finish this process I have started and think about the future. *My* future. Jeannie has a friend, Stefan, who runs a bed and breakfast with his partner Al, in Cape May, on the southern tip of the Jersey coast. How about she calls him and discreetly tells him that I'm seeking a peaceful getaway, having recently suffered the pain of a broken marriage? (More or less true, although the pain isn't for the loss of the marriage but the loss of what I have barely known. Except for with Mike, that is.) I knew it with Mike for those four years. That was the time I stepped out of the mould.

I was to think of Mike often on the drive to New Jersey. Jeannie could never have guessed how well I knew every turn in the highway, every place to stop en route. Those weekends, when Rosie was with her father Bob, Mike and I would take off, like excited teenagers, to spend romantic nights in one of Cape May's gingerbread boarding houses. I thought of Bob, too, and that young and innocent marriage of convention engineered by our parents. For ten terrifyingly long and isolated years we existed uneasily and unhappily alongside each other. Then Mike moved in next door and for the first and only time in my life, love arrived. Love with a capital L. She flew into my heart and made her home there. For four glorious years my heart sang. By day we worked, lusting side by side, barely able to keep our hands away from each other, until eventually one of us would drag the other into the bedroom. Often not making it as far as the bed, we would close the door on the world as, rolling on the floor, each hungry body devoured the other. That delicious taste of love's heady nectar as I drank in the smell, the touch and the feel. Always wanting to be in deeper and deeper, until that complete obliteration of self. Later, much later, we would fall asleep entwined. Safely in harbour for the night.

Now, back in Cape May, as I looked around the quaint, perfectly proportioned Victorian room with the pink roses on the wallpaper, the pink silk cover on the double bed and the rosy button-back repro chair, I remembered other rooms, other names. One wooden boarding house here was called Victorian Heart. That's why we had picked it. We were so soppy. Mike was an artist and it was here that he sold so many of his watercolours as mementoes to these unforgettable sunsets. Moments of pure magic as the sun dipping down casts her golden cloak upon the rippling ocean. With a few deft strokes, he would capture them with his pencil to be transformed with paint at home, bringing the finished picture with us the next trip.

Home was a small apartment with a north skylight on Lower Eastside in downtown New York. When we had first met, Mike had been house-sitting next door to Bob and me in Soho. I had been up on the roof tending my plants and wondering which of my three little black cocktail dresses I should wear that evening to a business dinner with Bob, when I heard a noise like a deckchair collapsing. Then a groan and a muttered curse. Peering through the foliage, I saw a lanky, dark haired, middle-aged man disentangling himself from a mangled chair and tipped table, with glass shards everywhere. Blood dripping from his hand.

"Can I help?"

He looked up and smiled that crooked smile that went right up into his eyes. And in that second I felt my heart turn over. It did a flip. It truly did. And it stayed flipped.

From that day I spent every afternoon on the roof and so did he. Greedily I drank in every detail and stored it away to memory. A priceless treasure to be carefully wrapped and saved for when those empty moments came. And those empty moments did come. Like now. Remembering the way his hair fell across his right eye. Those clear, direct brown eyes that had a way of knowing and from which I could hide nothing. The way they looked the first time we had made love, the intensity when we both realised we were drowning. Drowning in love. Sucked down into her depths from which there could be no turning back now that the tide had taken us.

The reality was hard. I was the respectable 30-year-old wife of a respectable young attorney and mother of a much beloved child, Rosie. I adored my child but not my husband. I had a settled, well ordered and well-moneyed existence. So the period of self-denial began. Mike went back to his own apartment and I tried not to see him. My newly awoken body ached with the passion so recently discovered inside myself. And just as the tears had flowed in these last weeks, so the longing had flowed then and I was powerless to stop it. The switch had been turned on and I couldn't turn the current off. Two weeks passed before I packed a bag, gathered Rosie up and landed on his doorstep. And I never left.

In some ways Bob was relieved. He bought me the house in Brooklyn while he moved into an apartment and began an affair with his secretary. Or perhaps he had been having an affair throughout the marriage? Who knows? He was happy for Rosie to be with me and he saw her most weekends. He was – is – a good father. My father puffed out his cheeks and disowned me, of course, and my cool English mother cried. But I didn't care.

And so began the golden period of Chloe Fairchild's life.

The sun seemed to shine every day, or so it seems to me, looking back now. Deeply contented, I glowed in this unexpected gift of love and warmth. After six months, we moved into my new house and Mike set his studio up in the room at the back with the north-facing window. We began to produce our own cards and prints of his paintings. The sunsets of Cape May, children playing on the shore, seabirds ducking and diving. Those shared memories of another time, another person. Where was she now? The woman whose body had trembled at the briefest passing touch from this one man? A man whose glance sent such a surge of desire roaring through my blood, causing me to blush furiously as my thighs throbbed so much, I thought people might catch them twitching beneath my skirt!

And here I am once again. Cape May five years on. Older – that's for sure. Wiser? Right now I am a jumble of tumbling thoughts. "Time to pull yourself together, Chloe." My shoes off, I feel the coarse grains of sand between my toes as I walk towards the setting sun and those years just melt away. That lean brown hand with the sensitive, artistic fingers that so firmly clasped mine, that long stride. The quick glance, the laughter, the hug. And that intensity. Almost as if we knew. With each year came a deepening of the bond that held us so tightly enmeshed each within the other. Until, that spring day came when I awoke to sunbeams and birdsong and, turning my head upon the pillow, gazed into Mike's open but now unseeing eyes. That was the day when my heart stopped and when it beat again it was never with the same rhythm. A massive brain haemorrhage, the doctor said. It would have been quick, he wouldn't have suffered much.

And so had ended the golden period of Chloe Fairchild's life.

Sitting on the edge of this first seashore resort in America, the scene is as vivid as if it were yesterday. One moment my man was warm in bed beside me, the next he was gone from me. Forever. I want to scream and shout and shake my hate at God. "*I hate you, God!* If there *is* a God!" But this burst of anger disappears almost as soon as it comes and I just want to run back to Brooklyn, climb back into bed and sink down under the covers again into that familiar place.

Am I losing the plot? But then if I don't know what the

plot is, how can I lose it? I know! Walking! I have heard that walking is good. I will make myself walk. And walk. And walk. So I just stride furiously on, oblivious of my surroundings. The stares. A slight, middle-aged woman, head bent, clenched expression, one bare foot in front of another, sandals dangling from my hand. Off the beach now. The beautiful gardens, the tree-lined streets, the ornate houses with their balconies and verandas passing unnoticed.

It's nearly dusk before I slow down, panting, and realise I have no idea where I am exactly. Stopping at a cutesy olde tea shoppe, I decide to go in and order a tea. The room is packed with tourists. I have to share a table with a tall, fair-haired Dutchman who's come to have a look at the architecture that is Cape May. On the wall hangs a picture of Cornelius Jacobsen Mey, his compatriot, who named the peninsula after himself.

My mind runs distractedly on and in and out and back to my father again. My father had paid me a visit and offered to take me back into the family home if I agreed to toe the line, do what I was told and conduct myself in a fitting manner. What line was he talking about? What *is* a fitting manner? He offered to pay for me to see an analyst. Something I should have done years ago, he said. Numbly I refused. Bob called and awkwardly put his arms around me as he asked if there was anything he could do. Do? What could anybody do? Unless they live in a black hole too. Do they observe daily life, detached, as if from some far away distant planet? Like watching through a gauze curtain. Only everyone else is on the other side. A place where there is nothing. No feeling.

In the face of this stony devastation, Bob took Rosie away for the weekend. I sold Mike's paints and easel and wound up the print business. I borrowed money and started the florists. Jeannie stood by me then as she has now. Laughter becoming a distant memory. The hole inside me dug too deep for tears. The new lines on my face etched too deeply to ever leave again. Life existed on automatic pilot. Real feelings seemed sort of squashed away somewhere. Once again I crept down into that jar and hid, making sure the exterior appeared as smooth and polished as I could for Rosie's sake.

Then, two years ago, Brett had presented himself at the door in answer to my advertisement for a lodger. An out-of-work actor, he used his acting skills to charm his way into my life when I was at my most vulnerable. Unfortunately, lightheartedness was all Brett had to offer. His big break never came but he didn't seem to mind too much as he slouched in front of the TV screen or slept late into the mornings. His hours in front of the bathroom mirror practising different facial expressions before yet another failed audition began to irritate. But then that day came when I snapped. Boiled over. Circuit blown. And now Cape May again...

"Are you feeling quite well?" The Dutchman startles me with his interruption.

"Why, do I look unwell?" I snap back at him, flustered. Then, sorry, I apologise, and later he walks me back along the shore to the boarding house.

That night I dream of Mike. I am to dream of him many times over the week but oddly this comforts me. Stefan watching over me like a mother hen with her troubled chick. I feel so uncertain. So afraid. So small somehow. Courage is what I need.

On the fourth day it begins to shower As the rain falls, so do my tears. Hollywood isn't in it. I give an Oscar-winning performance. Then, as I watch the windscreen wipers wipe to the tune of Ave Maria, the smallest bubble of laughter starts to well up from somewhere deep inside of me. It reaches my throat with a great gurgling laugh "You, Chloe Fairchild, are being ridiculous," I tell myself. "Stop this boring whingeing and get on with life."

And so it was. The healing began. I swam. I ate. I slept. By the end of the second week, I was ready to go back. I knew what I had to do. I think I know how to find myself again. I phone Rosie and we arrange to meet that night. I want to see that look of fear leave her face.

Chapter 2

"You've had a breakdown. I've been waiting for this ever since Mike died." Kindly Doc Brady peers at me over his spectacles a week later. A chest infection has taken me to his surgery. "I always knew Brett wasn't going to be the right man for you. Not after Mike."

"Not a break*down*, Dr Brady. More like a break*out*!"

(Just a scattered piece of jigsaw right now, but when fitted together again it would show a whole new picture).

"The straitjacket is off. The cage door is finally open and this bird is going to fly." As I laugh, rather too loudly, the poor doctor looks worried.

"What straitjacket, Chloe? Are you sure you're feeling quite all right? You've lost an awful lot of weight. I'm going to prescribe you an anti-depressant as well and then I think you should see a therapist. You need to work your way through this grief. You never did, you know." This last was gently said. An anti-depressant? But I don't feel depressed. Not the least bit. Not any more. As for a therapist – a new life will be my counsellor. He writes my name on another prescription and ticks a relevant box. Satisfied at having found a category for me, he visibly relaxes and now leans back in the worn leather chair.

"Thank you, Doctor, but I won't be needing this one, you see, I don't fit in a box. Never did." I smile sweetly and exit quickly before he tries to find another to squeeze me into.

Passing through the waiting area, I count at least twenty more boxes all waiting to be categorised, stamped and dated. *Monday 19th August 1991, Depression. Monday 19th August 1991, Heartburn. Monday 19th August 1991, Cancer.* Labels, sometimes life sentences, to be handed out each day. No wonder Doc Brady looks so careworn. Playing God obviously takes its toll.

That evening the face that looks back at me from the mirror is already one I barely recognise. So much thinner, yes, new hollows in my cheeks meeting those purple shadows under my eyes. Eyes, washed so often over these last weeks with salt tears, seeming faded. And lines. New lines. Dear Lord. Apart from those years with Mike, the first act of this play was such a mess. Time to clean up.

"I'll be away for at least three months," I tell Rosie later. "I'm going to visit your grandmother in England, and then I'll start travelling."

It was the 'growing through going places' slogan that did it. Like a thunderbolt, the billboard with its flying aeroplane and happy smiling faces hit me like a direct line sign from God himself. Just for *me!* That's *it* Chloe. *Go* to *grow.* Growing through going. I find I like the sound of it, the way it keeps reverberating around and around in my head. Growing through going. Growing through going.

Rosie starts to say something but changes her mind.

Instead her face goes tight. I know this is hard for her. I pull her to me and hold her close. Rosie, with Bob's big brown eyes, who tries so hard always to do and say the right thing. Rosie, who in a week's time is leaving to go backpacking around Australia. "Try to understand, darling," I say as I push a strand of hair away from her eyes and tuck it behind her ears. But from those eyes I see she doesn't.

It takes only a few days to find a couple to rent the house and with new energy I pack away clothes and treasures into the loft. Those pictures of Rosie as a baby, Rosie with Bob and me and later, Rosie with Mike and me on the beach at Cape May. Those pictures of Mike. Mike on the roof, in the studio, asleep in bed, one arm tucked under the pillow. I look at those familiar faces of the two people I love most in the world and for a moment a craving so deep and poignant overwhelms me. For just a split second time stops with the captured moment and I am caught in it. Then I sigh, because at the end of the day all I hold in my hand is a snapshot of the past to be lovingly packed away in an old tin trunk. How relentlessly the time clock ticks on! And now I must tick with it. Catch up and keep up. The little butterfly pendant Mike gave me stays out. When he died I had taken it off and wrapped it in tissue. It had been hidden at the back of a drawer. The sight of it each time I had looked in a mirror had been too much, the feel of it a constant reminder. But now I shall wear it as a good luck charm. Putting this delicate blue and silver enamel piece around my neck somehow makes me feel better. And sort of protected. A little piece of Mike travelling with me. And you know something? It feels good. The way it sits so neatly around my neck.

On Sunday evening, when Rosie, Jeannie and I finally sit down to a take-out pizza and a glass of wine, we are all exhausted.

"But Mom, you don't even know where you're going!" Rosie's tone is one of exasperation.

"Oh yes I do!" The words are out before I catch them, and they take me by surprise. Now I have started this, I've got to finish. "India," I add boldly.

Two heads now turn towards me. Mustn't falter. "India?" the two chorus together.

"Yes, why not?" India should be far enough away to start and extreme enough to change the picture. Create a new me. "With a backpack." I drop this in with what I hope passes for trendy coolness.

"But *why* India? Isn't that a bit drastic? And a backpack! It isn't safe for a woman to travel alone. Especially a woman of your age. And you haven't travelled anywhere except England. And that was years ago. You were a child. You don't know anything about India!" Rosie is now looking distraught. Jeannie is silent.

Drastic? Yes, that's why I chose it. Don't you two see? Drastic is what I want. Need. Drastic change. Besides, I don't like who I've become whilst living in a cage.

"And that's precisely why I'm going there. Because I know nothing about it. Oh, don't worry. Other people do it, so why not me?"

"Other people are half your age," mutters Rosie almost, but not quite, inaudibly.

Neither of them looks convinced.

And to tell the truth, there's a tiny bit of me that isn't either. Last night I dreamt of Mike again. Holding my hand, leading me through a street full of colour, a packed throng of people, cows and rickshaws all around us. Suddenly we were at wide steps leading upwards towards an ancient mosque. When I looked down at myself, I saw a golden silk sari shot through with threads of silver and intricate embroidered flowers covered with silver beads. A wedding sari! Mike turned and smiled right up into his eyes as they held mine. The heavy sensual smell of lilies hung in the air. I awoke smiling, the word 'India' on my lips and that exotic perfume lingering in my nostrils. So India it has to be. Besides, it feels sort of right.

I call Bob and let him know what I am doing. Then its Brett's turn. "Are you fit enough to go anywhere, Baby?" *Uh!* How I hate being called 'Baby'. Funny, isn't it, how a single word can be the cause of so much irritation. "Would you like me to come around?" he says in that appealing little boy voice. I cut him off before he can fully immerse himself in today's role.

"That won't be necessary, Brett, thank you. We need to talk, though, because I want a divorce as soon as possible." We arrange to meet in Gianni's coffee shop downtown the next day.

Before I go to bed that night, I search for the world atlas on the top shelf of the bookcase. Getting it down, I find the right page. Snuggling under the covers, Tabitha purring beside me, pink perspex clock ticking, I look at it. Now, let me see where exactly *is* India? Oh! It does seem very far away. Perhaps Rosie's right after all...

Over a cappuccino on the sidewalk café downtown, Brett and I agree to divorce amicably. Brett, the wide-eyed and bewildered small child. Kissing him on the cheek, I watch him walk away to his next audition and I know the doctor is right – he was never my type anyway. Using my cell phone, I call my lawyer and set the wheels turning. Then it's into the bookstore. Ten minutes later and I am heading for the travel shop to buy my air ticket to England, a copy of *The Lonely Planet Guide to India* under my arm.

That afternoon I help Rosie to fill her backpack, a very small bag. Why didn't I take note as I watched her put in a couple of tee shirts, spare shorts, one change of underwear and sunscreen? "I'll buy anything else I need over there, Mom." Why didn't I hear her? Then we strolled along arm in arm to the florists where Jeannie was still working. This stalwart, flame-haired friend who never let me down was going to take over the running of the shop. Now, as I watch her so deftly tying ribbon around a bunch of twelve hot house red roses for a tall, handsome young man, I breathe in those heady perfumes one more time and, closing my eyes for a second, I know that I will *never* be back in this glasshouse on the street corner. I am moving on.

And so the week flies on in a flurry. First, it's goodbye to Rosie who looks as uncertain as she did on her first day at school, only instead of a school uniform she is wearing shorts, tee shirt and hiking boots. We cling to each other. "Do be careful, Mom," she murmurs before she turns with characteristic courage and walks through into the departure lounge, looking back over her shoulder to grin quickly and wave. Then she and her friend Joanna disappear from my sight. "Be safe, sweetheart," I whisper to myself.

"Hard watching someone you love leaving, isn't it?"

I'm so deep within my own thoughts I haven't noticed

the tall grey-haired man who has been standing beside me and who now waves to a pretty blonde girl, presumably his daughter.

"Yes, very hard." And with a large lump in my throat I turn and leave the terminal building. Only two days left before Jeannie will be waving goodbye to me but strangely I don't feel wobbly any more. More excited somehow.

Wandering through the house early on my last morning, watching the sun rising over the city from the window of Rosie's old bedroom, coffee mug perched on the ledge, one pyjama leg tucked under me on the cushioned seat, I think of all the times I have done just this. Like the time when Rosie was six years old and pretty sick. I sat with her all night watching for the fever to break until, exhausted, I had fallen asleep in just this position. Now I know this will be the last time I sit here. This home belongs to the past. The time has come to let go.

A glance at my watch lets me know I'll have to hurry. I pull on the new blue jeans, white shirt and sneakers. No shorts or hiking boots for me! Those are in one of my big black cases. Unlike Rosie, I have two overstuffed cases and a holdall! With no clue yet what to take for India, I've piled far too much into my bags, but I can sort that out at my mother's. A knock on the porch door and the cab and Jeannie have arrived. Quick kiss for Tabitha, who is asleep on the counterpane; one last sweeping glance around and I fly down those stairs without a backward glance. I am on my way. So much life to catch up with!

* * *

As the plane turns and drops down low, releasing the wheels with a thud, the green English patchwork dotted with neat houses and ordered gardens shows itself beneath the patchy clouds. Bringing only a child's memory with me, I search back to the last time. Most of the last moments of *that* flight were filled with instructions on expected behaviour and my clothes had been straightened and tidied and my hair brushed back hard into a far-too-tight ponytail, any straying locks gripped back with a little metal clip with a pink enamel flower that scratched my scalp. I was wearing that dull but expensive green coat with the Peter Pan velvet collar, my hands forced into those little kid gloves that my mother found so chic and which I hated with a vengeance, the buttons on the wrist being so damn fiddly. So I had missed the view, however constricted, from the window.

As the plane jolts suddenly, lands, then taxies and comes to a standstill, the stampede for the exit begins, everyone seeming so certain in their movements, so sure of where they are going as they open the overhead lockers, collect their jackets and carrier bags. For just a moment I am that small child again, on my way to become a pupil at the enclosed convent school of the Sisters of St John. The same school my mother and her sister, Pamela, attended. Those wimple-clad and silent women locked away from the world behind electronically operated doors, high walls and metal grills. I was to join them. Part of my grooming for a conventional life: "Teach you etiquette and restraint. Show you how to curb those unruly emotions. Give you a set of values to live by." To me it was more like a punishment than a set of values. A punishment for taking a walk downtown to where the tramps rummaged through the garbage. A week later repeating the experience, my lunchtime bagel squashed in my pocket to be shyly added to their shabby bags of other people's throw outs. "Your mother and I have spent the last two hours being concerned as to your whereabouts. It is not fitting for a child like you to mix with those sorts of people. They could do you harm." How very quickly they divided my world into 'our sorts of people' and 'those sorts of people' – 'our sorts', for some unknown reason, assumed to be superior to 'those sorts'. Strange, because the short time I spent with the three rheumy guys and one old woman entranced me. Those grimy faces with the lost eyes, their alcohol breath, the bulging bags around their feet, and the strange pungent body odour fascinated me.

"Sit here, beside me, child."

The old woman, whose name was Dolores, gestured to the sidewalk step. Enthralled, I watched her go through the day's pickings: a half-rotten lettuce, a couple of tomatoes, day-old bread and some cheese rinds and lastly, an old torn shirt. "This will do me nicely, honey. Time I threw away the one I am wearing." The idea that you could have only one shirt to wear intrigued me. Fiercely I committed every detail to memory to write into my secret journal that night (I had already decided I was going to be a writer when I grew up): the lines, deep with dirt, on her round black face; the bright orange scarf tied around her head with the few wisps of grey escaping; one shiny earring; old trainers with one sole flapping; several layers of skirt or cloths tied around her waist; the man-size shirt hanging loose.

"I had a child like you once but I lost her. They took her away."

I watched as she incessantly packed and unpacked the bags, checking every item again and again, all the while mumbling to herself. (To stop her thinking? Hide the pain?) The youngest of the group was a boy of eighteen though to a ten-year-old he seemed quite old. I liked his emaciated poet's face with its high cheekbones, framed with the stubble of his blond beard. A scruffy ponytail straggled down his back between his thin shoulder blades, and his hands trembled slightly as they picked out butt ends which he put into his own grubby tobacco pouch. I remember watching as he put a hand into his ripped pocket, pulled out a small bottle and, unscrewing the cap, swallowed most of the contents. "That's Luke," Dolores had said, "been on the streets most of his life. Brought up in cardboard city." What was a cardboard city? for Heaven's sakes. Whatever it was, it sounded quite exciting but it was hard to imagine a whole city made from cardboard. That night I had tried to find cardboard city in the dictionary. I couldn't ask my parents, life on the sidewalk around the bins being a world away from our own clockwork routines.

Then, a week later a friend of my mother's spotted me as I squatted beside Dolores. My game was up. "Something has to be done about the child. First it's abandoned kittens she keeps bringing home, next it will be one of those tramps. We'll be run over with hobos. This has got to stop."

My sojourn with the nuns had been brief as I decided to join their silence and refused to speak at all. I hoped that I might fade away and die quickly. None of the other girls seemed to suffer from this same affliction. Some even expressed a desire to join the order when they grew up. The horror of watching pretty Sister Dominic's thick, chestnut hair being lopped off and the sight of her prostrated body upon the cold chapel floor, before her marriage to an invisible bridegroom, made me puke up in the toilet afterwards. The memory of her scattered curls being swept into a dustpan filled my nightmares. How could she give herself away to God like that? She didn't even know Him. Rumour had it that she had lost her fiancé in a car crash. Most people were handcuffed and frog-marched into this forced imprisonment. A loss of freedom their punishment for wrongdoing. Already the world seemed a crazy topsy-turvy place.

After only a term, the school doctor pronounced that he couldn't take responsibility for the pale and stick-thin child. The shadow of myself would only nod its head in response to his gentle questioning. "Are you unhappy, child?" Then, turning to Sister Ignatius: "This is ridiculous, Sister. The life this poor child is leading – that you foolish women are all leading – is completely unnatural. Shut away from the real world like this. You all ought to climb over the walls and enjoy yourselves. Let rip. What are you all afraid of?" His gruff tone was one of frustrated exasperation. Sister Ignatius blinked rapidly, swallowed and then blushed, a huge great swathe of red flooding her neck and face, before turning me quickly around and ushering me out of the heathen's presence. A week later I was put on a plane back to New York to be met by disappointed parents.

Now, waiting in the jostling aisle of the plane, I feel only relief that I am on my own with not a grown-up in sight to tell me what to do unless I ask them. A knot of tension tightens in my stomach as I check my bag for passport and driving licence for what must be the sixth time.

In little under an hour I have got myself together, am in a

26

hired car, map on the seat beside me, bags in the trunk, and whistling. "Don't be vulgar Chloe, it's *so* common." I hear my father's voice. Whistling, as commonly as I know how, I head for the hotel in a place called East Grinstead, where I shall spend the night.

Stretching, my toes, touching the end of the bed, I feel gloriously energetic next morning, so decide to take a walk into town before heading off to Lincolnshire and my mother. East Grinstead seems a quaint old town with its old stone almshouses and other Tudor buildings that lean over the high street. U Go Overland is situated halfway up Station Road. It's the window full of posters of exotic faraway places that pulls me into a small stuffy office smelling of stale cigarette smoke and empty except for a dark-haired man at the back of the office gnawing his fingernails whilst doing battle with some poor guy on the other end of the phone. When he sees me he shrieks down the receiver, "Can't talk any more – customer!" and bangs the phone down so hard that it falls off the table onto the floor. The agitated way he leaps up and bounds towards me shows me that this is a man under pressure. Or maybe he is just having a bad day. Before I can speak, he reaches for a packet of cigarettes, lights one and inhales deeply like a desperate man fighting for some calm. I notice how his hand shakes. This guy is highly strung, I guess.

"Hi, I'm Chloe. I'm thinking of going to India." *No, Chloe, not thinking, you are going to India.* "I mean, I'm going to India, er, that is when I know where to go..." I tail off lamely. Suddenly he is focused and alert, anticipating a possible sale. Cigarette between his lips, his right hand shoots out and clasps mine with a grip like the proverbial vice or a drowning man.

"I'm James, how do you do?" Then he holds out the cigarette packet to me and gestures towards the red plastic chair. "Coffee?"

I accept the coffee as I do the offer of a cigarette and, while he is banging around in the back, I leaf through the travel brochures scattered across the low melamine table with its overflowing ashtray. A wealth of colourful pictures and enticing choices as one country after another beckons. I am caught among the monkey temples and orange-robed monks of Kathmandu when James returns bearing two mugs of Nescafe and an opened packet of biscuits. "Biscuit?" he offers as he takes one out, takes a bite, and then abstractedly picks up his smouldering cigarette.

Between puffs and bites he tells me about the trips his overland company make to India. "These are some of the photos of the last group to go." And he picks up some snapshots that were hiding under a magazine. A varied group of faces squinting into the sun. An elderly man looking as if he is taking advantage of this photo opportunity to cup the left buttock of a nubile-looking eighteen-year-old brunette standing beside him with the startled look of a trapped animal. Well, I hope he isn't thinking of coming on my trip! Then I remember the small patch of cellulite recently appeared. The stretch marks! Not nearly young or juicy enough for an overweight and lecherous old man!

"That's Mr Hodge," says James, noticing the direction of my gaze. "Lively old man." And he runs his hand nervously through his hair. At the thought of all that wobbling flesh and arthritic heaving, I have to bite my lips to compose my face. What if these trips are really a wonderful cover for ancient gentlemen looking for impotent escapades? *What a bitch, Chloe, but isn't it great that a sense of humour is coming back?* I want to laugh out loud but James distracts me with: "We have another trip leaving shortly led by Sean O'Ryan. After a few days on your own in Delhi, you can catch the bus and drive to Kathmandu. Sean is a great guy, knows India like the back of his hand. Done this particular trip fifteen times now." I must say that the thought of travelling with others for at least a little while *is* quite appealing. "It will set you up nicely for the rest of your journey."

Before I know it I am caught up in his verbal trip, hand over my passport, pay him £800 and am outside on the sidewalk again, James promising to send my tickets and visa to my mother's address. He is at the door waving when I remember a question I wanted to ask: "Oh, by the way, how many will we be on this trip?" But he has already turned back inside and is scavenging on the floor behind the desk – probably retrieving the phone. Looking at my watch, I realise it has taken only thirty minutes to seal my fate. With mounting excitement I wander on up the street and step into Horizons, a rainbow world of brightly coloured swirling patterns on flowing fabrics. It's only a short time before I have made a hefty spend and emerge with numerous bags of completely superfluous floaty trousers, sleeveless cotton tops and trailing chiffon scarves. Who says retail therapy isn't good?

Freddie Mercury and I sing together 'Time Waits for Nobody' as I put my foot down on the motorway and flashback to the last time I sang along. Then it was Cleopatra with Andreas

Bocelli in her pasteurised organic milk bath. Was it really only five weeks ago? At this moment there is no hint of that hysterical woman. I wonder how Rosie is. Does she feel this same sense of growing anticipation? The same fluttering butterflies? God, Rosie, how I love you.

As Freddie and I joyfully warble away, the hours slip by. In no time I am off the motorway and mooching along the almost deserted country roads. Huge open green on either side. Not a hedge in sight. When the ancient stone mansion reveals itself between the pine trees on my right and I pass beside the old and bent iron fence, the imposing wrought iron gates and lodge house of Larkham Manor, the landmark my mother had told me to watch out for, I know I am nearly there. The racecourse on my left and soon I am in the market square, full of vegetable and fruit stalls today, and turning off for the Laurels. One of twelve red-brick houses built around an old courtyard in a tasteful complex for the over 50s. When my father died, my mother had packed up, sold up and moved back to England to live with her widowed sister. The Laurels is the largest house but even if it hadn't been, I would have spotted those two white heads bent over their tatting. Those two heads that look up at the sound of my uncurbed and exuberant honking of the horn. As I watch them bustling to their feet, I catch my breath. Will I be like this one day? Tatting? Just waiting for death to catch me? The thought makes me shiver.

"Chloe, sweetheart it's so good to see you!" My tall and still handsome mother holds out her arms. Her white hair is stylishly drawn back from her fine face with its dewy skin. At seventy-eight she looks wonderfully elegant still in a long beige linen skirt and long cardigan to match. Silver chains hang around her neck and bracelets around her wrists. Those expressive hands still so beautifully manicured and sporting pink pearly nails. Hands that have rarely known the feel of the earth or the washing of dishes, being more accustomed to gloves, handshaking, or – not nearly often enough – playing the piano. Before her marriage my mother had been a concert pianist. I catch my dishevelled head in the hall mirror. Oh my God! Can I really be her daughter?

No matter how hard I try, I can never stay groomed. All those endless business dates with Bob when, by the end of the evening, my untamed hair would have spilled a lock or two and my designer dress would be crumpled, as my skirt is now. Well, at least I don't have any breakfast coffee stains today. We hug. Oh, not one of those big warm, all-enveloping bear hugs – a 'tweed coat' hug, as Jeannie calls them – but a restrained embrace. Pamela hovers behind until it's her turn to draw another's body to her with the same restraint.

"How nice to see you again, Chloe. It's been a long time." Pamela's vowels are pure cut-glass English to my mother's softer, more drawn-out sounds. Older than my mother by two years, and walking stiffly with a stick, but with the same elegance and style in her red trouser suit, she moves forward to greet me. A perfect house, expensively decorated and of exquisite taste, from the antique furniture to the old style brass light switches. The sort of house I grew up in. A bit like living in a museum. Home, at the weekends and school holidays, had been a custom built English style Manor House with harbour views and every amenity. A place where you looked, observed, but "don't touch the artefacts in case you damage them". In case you might *feel* something. *feel* you want to hold them, stroke them, learn about them. Or, God forbid, even *love* them! But now, as I look around this perfectly appointed house, so beautifully arranged, I don't feel the slightest desire to aim a kick at them or scream "but what about *people*? These are all empty stupid objects!" as I so often did when small.

"We've put you in the room at the top," Pamela says and makes her way to the chair lift at the bottom of the stairs. Settling herself on the seat, she presses a button and starts to glide slowly upwards. The house is on three floors and my room looks over the backyard with its weeping willow and roses and tubs of bright geraniums. A green room with pale aqua wallpaper, a cream carpet and heavy silk curtains matching the walls. Off it is a small shower room with thick green towels and Floris toiletries filling a basket beside the hand-basin. A television, radio, telephone and Victorian watercolours complete this tranquil picture. Opposite my room is another, almost identical except it's all blues. On the floor below, my mother's and Pamela's rooms are linked by a large bathroom. I suppose Pamela and her husband had slept in separate rooms, passing through the bathroom to bid each other a chaste goodnight, their passion spent long ago, their most intimate moments those that could be heard from the bathroom. Toilet affairs? Impossible to imagine that Mike and I might ever have wanted to sleep in separate rooms. There was barely a single night in four years when we didn't make love at least once and we always slept in the shelter of each other's arms.

"I hope you have everything you need up there," says my mother as we sit down to a late meal of cold meats and salad. The silver candlesticks are polished and the mahogany table shines, lamps glowing softly on the side tables beside the deep apricot armchairs in this lovely sitting and dining space knocked into one.

"You've got thin, Chloe," Mother says later over coffee. Pamela has gone straight to bed and we hear her moving about upstairs. I see the wariness in my mother's gaze as she looks at me intently. "It isn't funny being on your own at your age, darling." *No.* And as I return her look I see that it isn't funny being left on your own at her age, either. I chatter brightly about my plans. For once she is silent. Can that be something close to understanding I see coming into her eyes? After a long deep silence she simply says, "You need to go." Then she gets up, drops me a shy kiss on top of my head, pats me awkwardly on the shoulder and leaves the room.

Following her a few minutes later I pause outside her door and knock softly. Already in bed, her face cleansed of makeup, glasses on her nose, she looks pale and exhausted as, propped against one of her own hand-worked cushions, she turns the pages of a book. Suddenly I get that feeling of a pupil in the headmistress's study as I blurt out "Thank you for being understanding", before turning quickly and climbing on up to my green and leafy room at the top.

For as long as I can remember I have always wanted wings that could lift me up and take me with them to far-off places, but my wings were clipped and I lost the freedom to fly. That night I was to dream again. Standing on a window ledge and looking down upon a lighted city, I heard my mother's voice: "You can do it, Chloe. Fly. Fly." As I launch myself and kick my legs, my mother's unexpected laughter tinkling in my ears, I fly above the lights before drifting down and waking up. *Oh, how I would love to be one of those spangled acrobats fluttering towards the stripey roof of a circus tent.* With this thought, I turn over and sink into a deep sleep until a gentle tapping at my door wakes me: Aunt Pamela with a cup of tea.

And so a contented and gentle week passes in browsing through the antique shops in Horncastle with afternoon tea and scones in a hotel, walks to the local shops, and feeding the ducks beside the stream that runs behind the house. Quiet days. Gentle days. We never speak about anything of significance as we relax in deck chairs on the patio sipping Earl Grey tea out of delicate cups. It is a leisurely time. A refined time. A time to be savoured. A time that will never come again.

Chapter 3

It is already Friday and my last afternoon. My mother slowly climbs the stairs and stands in the doorway watching me.

"A backpack?"

I am startled by her query as she looks at my cases and the myriad overspilling carrier bags that now litter the cool aqua room. What would my mother know about backpacks?

"Chloe you're mad!" Surprisingly, this seemed to be said with fondness. "You can't travel around carrying cases and bags. You have to minimize, dear. Let's go to Lincoln and see what we can find." The thought makes her look quite pink and excited. I don't like to tell her that a backpack was what I'd planned all the time and this afternoon was the one I had set aside to find one. Well, it doesn't take us long to get to Lincoln and somewhere near the cathedral we find the right shop. A large camping shop filled with equipment and clothes for every possible type of trip. My mother, incongruous in fuchsia long-sleeved silk, perches in the middle on a tall stool, surrounded by bags of all colours and sizes.

"I love this purple, Mom, don't you?" I say as I pick a

huge bag off the floor. It's got black straps and flaps and lots of side pockets.

"A little large to carry on your back all over India, darling, don't you think?" is my mother's wry comment as I rummage around among bags of every shape and size. Of course! Rosie, her tiny bag and one change of knickers! But then I am not Rosie. There are certain things a middle-aged woman needs to take, like nail polish and one of those raspy things to sand the feet and night cream and all the other basic essentials to help keep the beckoning crepiness (or is it creepiness?) of old age in check.

"Found anything?" the spotty, pony-tailed young man asks me.

"Yes, I hope so. I'm going backpacking around India and need a suitable bag."

He can't quite hide his look of surprised amusement. "I was there last autumn myself," says Spotty at last, recovering. "It'll be very hot indeed so you won't want anything too heavy." This, with a doubtful glance at my thin shoulders. Right up until now I haven't really given this trip enough serious thought, seeing it as some kind of life raft. I haven't even opened my *Lonely Planet Guide*. But now I know I need to inform myself. And fast.

"Try this." He holds out a dark green canvas bag, helps me on with it and adjusts the straps.

"That looks about right, darling," announces mother. (How would she know what's right, I wonder, not unkindly.) But now I bow to their superior knowledge and agree. Next, it's a torch, penknife, sunscreen, sun hat and padlock and chain. "I'm not into bondage!" slips out before I can stop it. Spotty looks towards my mother, embarrassed. She goes pink again. "Really, Chloe. You're embarrassing him," she chides as he goes off for the length of heavy chain he tells me I will need to fasten my bag, "for security". On his return, he patiently explains how I am to wind it around the green bag to secure the contents from thieving fingers. Enunciating carefully as if speaking to a child. "Now, a whistle. To use against assailants."

"What? Who would want to assail me?" Is he trying to frighten me? Stunned and a bit unnerved, I watch as the whistle is added to the growing pile. Where were all those floaty clothes going to fit in? The sleeveless see-through tops and trailing Horizon scarves? A mosquito net, insect repellent, map, water tablets, neck purse, money belt to wear under my clothes, and on and on. At this rate I'll be lucky to fit my toothbrush in, let alone my lipstick and nail polish remover. The thought of carrying all this on my back is exhausting.

"Oh, just put everything in the bag and I'll carry it on my back now. I may as well get used to it."

Up until this moment my mother has looked relaxed and amused but now she pales. "No, Chloe," she says firmly, "I'm not walking through the city with my middle-aged daughter wearing a backpack. You're not in India yet."

So, laden down with packages, we leave the shop, bid farewell to the bemused Spotty and make for the chemist where I am to buy a first aid kit. "Don't forget the syringes!" is his parting shot.

"I'm not planning on sleeping with anyone or doing drugs, so will these be really necessary?" I ask the starched assistant behind the counter of the drugstore nearby.

"I should hope not," is my mother's faint riposte. "Really,

Chloe, no one would think you're a grown up woman and mother to an eighteen-year-old." This last is meant to be said *sotto voce*, but her voice carries and the assistant gives me a withering look. Agreeing. My mouth buttoned tight, I watch as the syringes are added to the already overfull bag.

"Well, that was fun." My mother looks stimulated as, surrounded by our purchases, we collapse into a tea shop, all oak panels, starched white cloths and Victorian-looking waitresses, wearing those frilly half aprons. Little cakes and dainty sandwiches garnished with watercress and served from a sort of tiered wooden cake stand. Thin china cups of smoky Lapsang Suchong. Looking across at my mother's flushed face, I wonder about her life. All those years with a dominant male, life revolving around his every whim. Did she lose herself somewhere too? Before I can stop myself, I reach out and clasp those beautiful ringed hands, now folded and neatly resting on the tabletop.

"I hope you've had a happy day. Thank you for helping me." For a split second she holds my eyes, squeezes my hand, then looks away, embarrassed.

"Please will you help me decide what clothes I should take with me. You know how I never have the right things. You always know what to wear. You've always looked so good, Mom," I plough on.

"Thank you, Chloe. Always so impulsive!" Her head gives a gracious dip in my direction. "Of course I'll help, but I've never been backpacking around India, you know. One concert tour of Europe is hardly the same as India." Smilingly.

"Concert tour around Europe? Mom, tell me. Please." I

want to know more. To get to know the woman my mother really is, was. Before it's too late. We begin to feel comfortable with each other in a way we never have before and the next hour passes swiftly as I listen to this woman I am seeing for the first time, recalling those years so full of talent and hope. Tea grows cold and cake is left uneaten. With passion she recollects concert halls, concertos played, countries visited. The words fall from her lips in a seemingly endless torrent. Her eyes sparkle. Spellbound, I could just sit here forever caught up in the web of this young and promising musician sitting opposite me, as she plays to packed concert halls and standing ovations. Laughing, she remembers the stage door Johnnies, their Afghans on leads, tossing a coin to see who would get to walk her home. The theatres rained flowers, it seemed, and the florists grew weary of delivering so many bouquets. "To a rising star who brings not only her great talent but her exceptional beauty to her playing." And my mother laughs. The quote of just one infatuated critic who craved her hand in marriage.

"But, Mom, what happened? You didn't really give it all up for Father, did you?" I ask her in a moment of almost breathless pause.

A stupid question. The animation drains from her face, the mask takes over and she becomes again the smooth and polished woman. The mother I have always known. "There are some questions best left unanswered, Chloe." And she plucks at a tiny loose thread on the edge of the tablecloth. Now it's my turn to feel awkward and distressed at breaking the spell. As I help her to her feet, all I see again is a gracious, elderly lady inclining her head to the waitress before sweeping out in style.

We go straight back to the camping shop as, feeling humbled, I agree to buy the extra padlock Spotty has suggested, though heaven knows what for. Right now I would agree to anything to bring back the animation. That sparkle and laugh. The intimacy between us. Just about to close, he is annoyingly amused to see us again so soon and goes off to fetch a larger one "for locking your door at night". Locking my door? Who is going to try and get into my bed? I can't imagine. I squash the thought before it leaves my lips. What sort of country am I going to? Obviously one of predatory males – or is this Spotty's idea of humour?

"You may want to consider veiling up." He and the padlock are back and he now drops this gem.

"Veiling up?" Mother looks startled and I try to pretend I haven't heard.

"Well, you know, an attractive… I mean blonde…" Now it's his turn to look discomfited. "It's not always a safe place, especially at night. Some women prefer to wear long trousers or skirts and cover their heads with a shawl…" He trails off and I am pleased to watch his face go red.

"I see," said my mother. Although I can't imagine that she does because I don't. See, I mean. Surely this is going way over the top? What is wrong with sleeveless tops and thin trousers? Trailing chiffon scarves?

"Will you be going to Delhi? There's a place I can recommend where you can buy a Punjabi suit really cheaply!"

Punjabi suit? Well, I'm not going to give him the satisfaction of thinking I don't know what he means. Now it's my mother who charms him, writing down the address for Punjabi suits, discussing clothes, climate etc. Leaving them both to chat, I take down a guide book and flick through. Religious violence, political turmoil, a caste system still happening and the modern day equivalent of female infanticide! A nervousness creeps over me and then Spotty is beside me. "Page ninety-five, madam, the section on women travellers." He takes the book, swiftly finds the page and jabs at it with a stubby freckled finger. I grab it back and snap it shut but not before I've seen something about "Eve teasing" being inappropriate body groping. Better not tell my mother about that one! Right now I don't know how my body feels about being touched, let alone groped, because it feels like it's gone into hibernation. I have no desire to run my hands over anyone else's body either. That wild bodily abandonment, met with the same exuberance. The soaring flight to the crescendo where two makes one. Memories of another time. Another woman. That part of me blocked off, shut down, the morning I looked into those dear familiar but unseeing eyes for the very last time. The weekly couplings with Brett brought a healthy ejaculation for the two of us but my light switch remains most definitely off. No, I don't think I'll be going in for any body groping sessions somehow. I put the book back on the shelf.

Trying to imagine how Eve might have looked at Adam before their apple episode, whilst following my mother, who is leaving the shop, I collide with the door. My exit ruined, I watch the huge grin spreading across Spotty's obnoxious face as I hurry to catch up. A walk through the cloistered gardens of the cathedral, flowered with plants named after the Virgin Mary and even the pagan goddess Venus with her Venus Comb. Mystic Roses, Our Lady's Thimble, Laces and Ribbons, Smocks and Mantles mingling their scents and bringing balm to my embarrassment. By the time we reach the car, I am fully recovered.

Later that night, reading in bed, I realise I have got it all wrong. It's the Adams who do the unwanted teasing and provocation. Not the Eves. Oh, shit!

Earlier in the evening I had tipped all my purchases, my Horizon bags and my suitcases, onto the thick cream pile carpet of my mother's bedroom. This meant that neither my mother or Pamela would have to climb up the last flight of stairs to the top of the house. My mother takes charge and Pamela watches as they make me parade in the different outfits, twirling in front of the walnut cheval mirror to comments from one or the other: "Try the rose linen top with those cream trousers" or "Oh no, that won't work". Looking at the dark green backpack and the huge pile on the carpet, it's obvious that Rosie got it right.

"Let's put all the essentials in first and see what room you have left," Pamela suggests. Looking from one to the other and around this disordered room, I realise they have never been in such a mess as they hold up one garment after another. Soon I am just parading for the sake of it in unsuitable but pretty clothes. But eventually it's time to stop when Mrs Plover, the part time help, puffs her way upstairs to let us know, rather grandly, that "dinner is served, Madam". I run upstairs collect some underwear and finally we pack my bag together.

"Haven't you anything less skimpy, dear? You're not staying in five star hotels." I think of the greying bra and dull knickers of a life just past and shove the lacy new thongs down the side of the bag with a flourish.

"Must be so uncomfortable to wear," is Aunt Pamela's

contribution. Only one pair of floaty trousers. "Put those on top. Minimize creasing. You'll travel in the others, won't you?"

The penknife and whistle are put in the side pockets. By the time the first aid kit and all of Spotty's other recommendations are in, there is just the smallest space left for my camera and wash things.

"There, let's go and have a glass of wine or we'll be in trouble with Mrs P. I don't want to upset her by keeping her waiting. She's a good sort." Overplump, homely Mrs P, her swollen ankles overflowing onto the extra wide orthopaedic sandals, her floral overall stretched tight across the ample bosom, is obviously an OK person. All our servants had always been treated with deference and understanding, even if they were rarely given their proper names. Did Chef have a real name? I used to wonder. Was Gunner, who kept the harbourside garden, polished father's shoes and cars, always Gunner or did his mother know him by another name? Chef had once run amok with the carving knife and had to be calmed down by my mother, who took it from him, lead him back to the kitchen and closed the door behind them both. My ear, pressed tight against it, caught the general gist. Something to do with the pantry door having been left open. Meat covered in bluebottles. "He's an artiste, George. Just overreacting," she later explained to my irate father, who'd had to wait an extra ten minutes for his lunch. But my mother was an "artiste" too. Did she really have an artist's temperament behind the cool exterior? For now, her voice sounds satisfied as I pull the straps together and close the top. They both look completely exhausted but oddly contented as we make our way downstairs towards Mrs P's delicious cooking smells, which are rising up to meet our nostrils and stir our senses. Aunt Pamela, gliding down on the stairlift, is the first to reach the hallway.

"Chloe, is that you, darling?" my mother calls as I pass her bedroom door on my way to bed. She is propped up with my *Lonely Planet Guide* to inform herself and fill me in with bits of information that she thinks I may find useful. "Remember to make sure the caps on the bottles of water you buy are properly sealed and haven't just been refilled, won't you? And don't forget to make room for toilet paper in your bag. Can't have you using your hand," she says with distaste. Before I can reply she rushes on, "You know, Chloe, you have a natural grace so it doesn't really matter what you wear or how untidy you are. You've always looked pretty, if a bit untidy sometimes," she smiles. I am nonplussed. "You see, at my age I have to buy expensive designer clothes to even look passable any more." *Yes, growing old must be hard when you have been such a beauty.* Well, for a woman of her age, she is still beautiful, handsome. She goes on quickly. "I'm sorry Mike died, Chloe." I am completely shocked for a moment as neither my mother or my father ever met Mike or referred to him by name from the day I left to live with him. But if this is the olive branch, it's too late now. Mike is dead. He's dead. Gone. I don't know what to say so I switch off her bedside lamp and bend to kiss the pale shrunken cheek lying there against the pile of pillows. Stumbling up the stairs, that childhood abyss of aloneness and hunger coming with me. Hunger to reach out and touch the very edges of existence.

Saturday comes in with another bright and clear sky. James from U Go Overland rings early to let me know my ticket and visa are there. I tell him I will call by later in the afternoon. Strangely, right now, I find it's a wrench to leave these two elderly women. The sunlight makes them seem so vulnerable, their wrinkles more obvious, their joints moving more stiffly. I feel glad they have each other. I can see tears appearing in my mother's eyes and she turns her head away to concentrate hard on a pink geranium in a pot by the front door. Even Aunt Pamela's voice trembles slightly as she murmurs, "Goodbye, dear, it's been so lovely to see you again after all these years." Will I ever see them again? India suddenly seems so very very far away. I long to rush to my mother and tell her that I love her. Suddenly, I want to throw my arms around her as I throw them around Rosie. Hold her tight. Just this once. But looking at the stiff back bent over the flower, I know it really *is* too late. The words just won't come out. Our easiness in the teashop is gone. Awkwardness is back.

Sadly, I climb into my car and drive away. "Write won't you, darling?" catches on the breeze and travels with me. I put Freddie back into the slot with a hard bang, turn the volume up, put my foot down and roar down the motorway back the way I came.

James isn't in the shop. In his place is a fair young man whose name turns out to be Claude. He waves an envelope at me. "Got it – it's all here, everything's in order. Coffee?"

Yes, I could do with a coffee. To tell the truth I am feeling worn out with driving and all that old emotional childhood stuff. I say no to the Camel cigarette he now offers me. He goes out the back and brings out two steaming mugs along with a small brown paper package, which he puts down on the table along with the ticket envelope. "Give that to Sean, will you? He's waiting for it." Then he turns away to fiddle with something on the desk. Before I can comment he carries on, "There's a guy coming all the way from Australia, you'll probably meet him in Delhi, his name is Jim. Got a picture of him here somewhere." He turns over piles of correspondence and finally comes up with a photo of a tall, pleasant-looking, middle-aged man wearing a navy blue polo shirt. Well, that's all right then. At least I know what one of the group looks like.

I have a very early start tomorrow but before I go back to the hotel there is one more thing I want to do. Looking at the instructions my mother has given me, I take Ship Street out of East Grinstead and wind my way along a narrow country road, heading towards West Hoathly. West Hoathly is an enchanting old village, houses all of stone, and those windows of tiny panes. Mullion windows, I think you call them. I am looking for the church, which is easy enough to find, standing opposite the old pub and surrounded as it is by ancient tombstones. There is the lych gate she told me about. It has a kind of wooden porch over it. A huge yew tree standing guard casts its shadow over the stone flagged path and momentarily obscures the magnificent view of rolling farmland.

Lifting the heavy latch on the old church door, I step into the coolness and take in the ancient font, the wooden pews with their needlepoint kneelers and the stained glass windows. Time unravels and I can see my mother as a young and startlingly beautiful young bride. A stark contrast to the pale and stiff looking woman I left behind only this morning. I breathe in deeply the smell of the wax candles, the flowers. In my ears I can hear the sound of organ music. And in that moment, for some reason, I want to weep for her.

GROWING THROUGH GOING

Chapter 4

I just know I can't be dreaming! The blast of hot air slamming into my body knocks my breath away. It is early still in New Delhi, only 6am. But already it feels like a wet and steaming blanket is smothering me. As I take the rail of the aircraft steps, the feeling that is beginning to become familiar returns. A sort of churning excitement all mixed up with just a tinge of anxiety around the edges. Like waiting for a first date to arrive. That moment you have been anticipating all day getting closer by the second! But in this instance my preparation has been a lifetime and my date is a country, not a man. The exploring not of the contours of a new male body and mind but those of a new map and culture. A quick touch to the butterfly around my neck and somehow Mike is here. Right with me. That long brown hand in mine. I swear I really feel that quick squeeze of encouragement and response. Can I really believe this? I am almost halfway around the world. And, perhaps, halfway to remembering whom I really am.

"*Namaste.* Please to open this package, madam." The customs man along the green channel indicates the small brown paper parcel that Claude from U Go Overland gave me for Sean. It was without a thought that I had taken the green channel and now the contents of my neck purse and backpack lie scattered all over the table. My mother and Aunt Pamela's carefully rolled clothes are adrift and mixed up with first aid kits and all the other bits Spotty had recommended. For a split second I panic and for the second time the breath nearly leaves me. My lungs thump against my rib cage in their struggle for air. Perspiration trickles down my back as a huge wad of English money is tipped out of its brown paper for everyone to see. How could I have been so stupid? Rosie would never have been so foolish. Why didn't I look inside? Why did I never give it a thought? Thank God it is only money! Relief drains me of what feels like my very last drop of energy.

"Not a good idea to carry so much money, madam!" scolds the man as he counts out £2000. Several men seem to be hanging around and staring at us but there are not the huge crowds I had imagined.

"No. You're quite right. Very stupid of me." And with my heart thumping in unison with my lungs, and my hands shaking, I quickly stuff the notes into my purse and put it around my neck again. Then, in one swift movement, I shovel my clothes back into my bag and hurry away towards the exit sign, a small man following behind me.

"Taxi, madam? I carry your bag to the taxi, madam."

"No thank you, I can manage." Still shaken, I shift the recently restuffed backpack to feel more comfortable on my shoulders remembering Spotty's doubtful glances at their thinness.

"I have very good taxi, madam. Very clean."

"I'm sure you do." I am trying to remember what it is the guide says about taking taxis. With the driver welded to my side, I exit the building and once again the ferocity of the humid air hits me. Feels like every pore of my body is starting to open and seep.

"This way, lady," he says, pointing to the most clapped-out mechanised rickshaw standing in a long line of rickshaws. Oh well, what the hell! It *is* painted yellow and that makes it OK for tourists.

"Look, how much will you charge me to take me to the hostel on the Jai Singh Road?"

"I very, very cheap, madam!"

"Yes but just how much is cheap?" I insist, remembering the caution to establish a price before setting off.

"Please, lady." He is almost begging.

Now we are joined by another man and then another. All of them seem to be small of stature and with bare feet. It seems like a few seconds only before there must be twenty of them all jostling for business. Determined hands reach out to take my bag off my back and I am pulled towards them. *For heaven's sakes, how long is it since so many men surrounded you, Chloe? If ever? Try to keep a sense of humour, honey.*

"This way, madam."

"Come, madam. I have *best* taxi."

"I know good hotel, lady."

"Beautiful lady like you, madam, needs *best* taxi."

"I change money too. You want to change money, lady?"

"I take your bag." And a shifty looking man with a squint tugs again at my backpack.

Glancing quickly down at the one welded to my side, I notice he has two toes missing and there's a huge lump on one heel. His feet are covered in grey dust and his thin trousers are none too clean. His eyes are all moist and pleading, like the eyes of a starving dog, as he touches my arm. As yet more would-be taxi drivers start to wander towards us I decide to give in, seeing it as the easiest, if not the only option, right now.

"OK! I go with you. You were first!"

I hope I am making the right decision as I get in, feeling a little nervous, and sit very upright on the seat, my bag beside me, so as not to miss anything. We set off for the Jai Singh Road and it's only then I realise that I am through the airport and no beggars in sight.

Two minutes later: "Are you married, madam?" Singh (for that was his name) turns in his seat and looks at me. I am startled, for I wasn't expecting this.

"Yes." (Said most definitely.)

"Do you have children, madam?"

"Yes, I most *definitely* do!"

"What about your husband, madam?"

"He is at home, er, with the children."

"This cannot be true, madam"

"Why not? Why can it not be true?"

"If you were married, madam, you would not leave your husband or your children. So it is not possible that you have children or a husband. I myself am looking for a wife, madam."

What? Somehow I don't see this conversation going anywhere. What was it I read about starting inane conversations with men? Something about it being a turn on? Not Adam teasing, surely? Well, first lesson learnt. No use lying. Very quickly I am to learn that it doesn't matter what I reply. But this time I am saved from a further marriage proposal by the Sacred Cow, who chooses this moment to amble in front of us and across this spacious British-made road. Singh swerves violently, toots the horn, and I am thrown back into the seat, where I try hard to relax. Quite unsuccessfully. We are driving alongside a park where I can see monkeys running between the trees, cows standing around stone monuments and huge crows and vultures routing among the garbage on the roadside. Elegant polo ponies with smart riders in short-sleeved shirts exercising early before the even greater heat takes over, the grey dust rising from their hooves.

"I take you to very good hotel, madam." Singh interrupts my thoughts.

"Now look, Singh..." Shall I try my Miss Jean Brodie voice? I loved that movie. "I insist that you take me to the hostel." At this he looks suddenly sad and despondent. I don't understand that Singh and his friends are given extra *baksheesh* to take visitors to particular hotels.

He is sulking but Jean continues. "If you persist with this I shall climb out at the next traffic lights." Brave words but they do seem to do the trick for he remains silent and I lean back again to take in all I can see around me.

Wow! I am tired and – disaster! – the hostel doesn't have a room for me. I am glad Singh isn't here or I would be whisked off to goodness knows where. Seeing him look so despondent on our arrival, I gave him a few extra rupees. "I come back soon? Take you on tour of Delhi? You like visit Bazaar? Most ladies like Bazaar. Maybe you buy carpet? I am waiting you." His last word, "tomorrow?", wafted behind me as I walked away from him and up the pathway towards the entrance.

Once inside I join a throng of young people queuing at a small desk behind which the two young men are dealing quietly and politely with requests for rooms. A slow fan rotates the stifling and smelly air and a large unidentifiable green plant wilts sadly in a brown clay pot. I don't need to look around far to know that I am the oldest woman here by many years. Feeling quite exhausted, I put my backpack on the crowded floor in the hall, sit on it, my back against the wall and fall almost instantly asleep.

Some two hours later a gentle hand on the shoulder wakes me and a young Indian girl in a bright yellow sari tells me, "We have a room ready for you now." The room is small, airless and very basic. It's also four floors up. Looking back now, I don't believe there was even a window. Just another old fan whirling slowly around above the iron bed with the greying sheets. The shower block is one floor down. No, I won't shower, as I don't believe I shall ever find the energy to climb all those stairs again. I strip down to my new and lacy (though I am not sure if they are sexy and, right now, I don't care) bra and very uncomfortable thongs. *OK, Aunt Pamela, you win. Comfy sensible knickers will have to go on my shopping list.* Lying at the bottom of the bed directly under the fan, arms and legs stretched wide to catch any spare air that might come my way, I try to get back to sleep again. Shall I ever be able to function in this humidity?

I must have dozed off because a loud knock on the door brings me back into this room and myself. Struggling back into my floaty clothes, I groggily make my way to the door.

Sean O'Ryan is a stocky man in torn jean shorts and a

sleeveless singlet with more than a glimpse of hairy chest. He holds out a firm hand and as he does so, he asks for the package of money. "I need it urgently for repairs on the bus," he explains. Why, I think I quite like the look of him with his tousled hair, green eyes and strong physique. Kind of reassuring, I guess. A man I will feel safe with. He is in a hurry to leave but just before he goes, turns and asks if I would like to meet for a curry later this evening. Sounds like a great idea, but will I ever get myself together? Leaving my clothes on this time I lie down again and remain in this supine position for the rest of the day.

Down in the foyer that evening it's hard to believe it's the same man. Gone are the torn shorts and in their place a pair of cream chinos worn with a deep blue silk shirt. Brown open leather sandals complete an attractive picture. What a surprise! A short walk along a crowded and malodorous back street and we're in a small and dingy restaurant where cleanliness is not a top priority, a long narrow slit of a room with two bare wooden trestle type tables and assorted chairs with string seats. The owner, who is also the cook, seems to know Sean well and welcomes us with a big beaming smile. It is he who ladles the fragrant vegetables out of the steaming pot sitting on the old blackened cooker at the end of this low-ceilinged room. Flies hover as we eat a curry of vegetables accompanied by rice, chapattis and relishes of all kinds. Two slim youths, who turn out to be his sons, hang back talking, picking their teeth, and exclaiming over pictures in the newspaper that lies on the small counter towards the far end. Sean is a delightful dinner companion as he talks confidentially about his travels around India and I realise I shall have a competent guide for the first few weeks of my

Indian adventure. Difficult to guess his age but he is spot on with mine, which is a little disappointing! I had thought I was beginning to look better again what with the weight loss, the freshly highlighted hair and even an artificial tan. In spite of the creasing, the swirly red skirt suits me. Sean turns out to be thirty-seven, unmarried and not forthcoming about his past. When I drain my coffee cup he jumps up, ready to leave immediately, asks for the bill, and before I know it we are back on the street, his friend at the restaurant affectionately waving goodbye from the door. "You will come back again, yes? I cook you very special dish."

Strolling back along the way we came Sean surprises me with "Chloe, would you like to meet again tomorrow evening? We'll go to a different curry house."

"Why, I think I would. Thank you."

Outside the hostel we shake hands. As he walks away he stops, remembering something. "By the way, don't go out in that skirt tomorrow, will you? Wearing a drawstring skirt like that is like walking around in your underwear here! The women often wear them as petticoats in Rajastan." And he walks on and disappears into the dusk. Talk about a pricked balloon at the end of the party! All the other times I ever felt like this now roll into this one moment. I feel wretchedly embarrassed.

A tug on my sleeve quickly jolts me out of this self-pity. "You like taxi, madam? Tour of Delhi now?" And there, looking up at me, is my friend Singh. Poor Singh! He sure knows how to pick his moments! Does he always have this effect? I collapse into a fit of the giggles at the absurdity of it all. "No Singh I do *not* want a taxi, thank you!" (Nor a husband.) I leave him lurking under the trees by the hostel gate. Over the next few weeks Singh will always be lurking around the hostel gate or setting himself the task of following me or someone else just in case we might need his taxi or even a husband.

It's thanks to Singh that I climb the stairs with laughter in my heart. I am not going to let a chance remark spoil my first evening. Lying down completely naked this time, I listen to the night sounds coming from the street four floors down. Sometimes it's a voice calling as if the sound came from between cupped hands and sometimes settling sort of noises, scraping sounds and the odd groan. Tomorrow evening I must investigate but for now exhaustion overtakes me again and sleep is what I crave.

With wide-open eyes and a shiny glistening face (my new fashion accessory), I nervously set out to wander the streets of Delhi early the next morning. Perspiration runs in rivulets from every bodily crease and fold but after a few moments nothing can dampen the thrill of discovering these streets, revelling in the sights and feelings that leap at me from every corner, every shop doorway, every stall and every passing face. So many sensations, so many perfumes hitting all my senses at once, as I duck down under the road and into the subway to the bazaar. The Palika Bazaar is a labyrinth of underground roads lined by lit open-fronted stalls and shops. Here there is a stronger odour of urine overlaid with a thin disguise of incense. My blonde hair is making me a target for lots of staring curiosity from both sexes. Shy giggling behind veils delicately held up across the lower part of the face by hennaed hands. Dark brown eyes sparkling with laughter at this white giant. So conspicuous in my Horizon type Indian trousers and top, I can't wait to swap them for something more discreet. It's not easy to find the right shop because there are so many, but with Spotty's piece of paper, saved and safely stowed away in my back pack by my mother, and a few enquiries, I eventually locate it.

Folded upon the shelves in this small, dark but cooler space is a miscellany of cloths, saris and clothes of every hue, from the deepest shades of purple silk to the purest white cotton lawn. Colour spills everywhere you look from the *salwar kameez* hanging from the low ceiling to the turquoise mirrored shawls tumbling from the pile on the small counter in the corner.

"*Namaste*. Welcome, madam. What can I show you?"

A small white-robed man with a white cap on his grey hair peers through the folds of the hanging clothes. Like an actor parting the rich curtains for the play's epilogue, he now steps in front of me, the paleness of his robes emphasising his lined and sallow skin.

"Oh, er... A friend of mine, Kevin Brown, recommended me to visit you." So Spotty is really a Kevin?

"It will be an honour, madam," he murmurs, bowing in reverence and folding his hands together as if ready for prayer.

"I'm looking for a Punjabi suit." Or two or three, as it turns out!

What fun, as for the next hour I try on suits of every size and colour and even a scarlet sari, its exquisite silk shot with golden threads. In the darkest corner a piece of fabric hanging from a bamboo pole serves as my changing room and a hand-held mirror as my looking glass. How many silkworms made this and how hard must they have worked, I wonder, as I pull out bale after bale of kaleidoscopic silks, scrunch my hands into the crinkled shawls, throw jewelled stoles around my shoulders and lose myself in this magical world of myriad colours that I have entered from the dingy underground street. And always there is another, yet more beautiful to touch and admire. Mr Raj is quiet and unobtrusive as he allows me to take down what I want to look at or try on, occasionally rescuing a stacked bale as it threatens to topple. As I turn to ask, for the umpteenth time, if I can remove another crisp white suit from the flat pack, another customer comes in. A man also seeking a Punjabi suit.

"*Namaste.*" We all join our palms together and bow at each other in what I quickly learn is the customary greeting. The three of us now jostle together in this small intimate space when finally the inevitable happens. The ceiling-high bales of bright silks start to go. As one we leap forward, hands outstretched, to catch the falling rainbow.

"Oh my God!" I cry.

"Goodness gracious!" adds the gentleman customer.

"Not to worry," soothes Mr Raj as the colourful waterfall rains around us and brings with it echoes of childhood.

"Oh no, Chloe, not again!" I tell myself as I trip or knock something over. Even now, I only have to look at a dress for it to fall off the hanger! Rosie hates shopping with me and Brett used to use it as an acting opportunity, as he would raise his eyes to heaven in mock horror, and then to the young shop assistant, as yet another dress slid to the floor. Now I feel this latest topple must somehow have been my fault.

"I'm so sorry. I do hope it wasn't my fault."

Mr Raj surveys the yards of cloth that have risen suddenly into something resembling an untidy pyramid in the middle of the floor, smiles a trifle wistfully I think, and says, "Oh no, madam. Not to worry. Soon have this cleared up." As he speaks he begins to deftly draw the fabulous silks apart, lovingly tames them quickly into shape again and starts a new stack of bales. I am surrounded by so much glory here. Such beauty in these iridescent colours now in an unfurled sea all around me. Soon to be rolled and wrapped again and tidied up and stacked into piles as high as the ceiling.

Looking at the patient back of Mr Raj, I think it's time I got out of here. So I pick out the cream cotton lawn with the long, self-embroidered tunic and trouser cuffs. I can't make up my mind between the blue and the green so I'll go for them both! Next a delicious crinkle shawl in varying shades of blue and another bright green silk, which I really can't resist. Finally a Kashmiri multi-embroidered fine wool shawl, which I shall never wear in this heat but it's far too beautiful to leave behind. Thanking Mr Raj, I join my hands in greeting, bow and regretfully leave.

Carrying bags doesn't help what little air there is to circulate around the body so it's a great relief to get back to my room. My neck purse is wringing wet and so are my passport and notes. Carefully separating them, I put them on the wooden bedside table to dry out a bit. Swigging water from my bottle, I decide to leave the rest of today's sightseeing until this evening, when it might be a little cooler.

Later, its Sean's turn to look surprised when I enter the foyer. "Very nice too!" he quips, and joins his palms together. "*Namaste!*" Checking to see if he is mocking after his parting remark of last night, all I meet is cool appraisal in those green Irish eyes. I've chosen the blue Punjabi suit and crinkle shawl, which I have arranged around my shoulders as Mr Raj showed me.

"Blue matches your eyes – you should wear it often". Sean startles me with the compliment and I blush. "What's the matter with you, Chloe, can't take a compliment?" This somehow makes it worse. I feel ill-at-ease and pathetic so I head for the door and hope he is following.

"Hey, what's the hurry? Haven't you eaten yet today?" Laughing at me, he holds the door open. Tonight it's a Lebanese restaurant, all red plush and soft lights, snow white tablecloths and sparkling cutlery. Green trailing plants and pictures of various Hindu gods hang on the flocked walls. The manager welcomes Sean like a long lost friend as he settles him under the protective arms of Shiva. Sean indicates the long and laden table stretching along one wall and covered with the silver lidded dishes. As the waiters lift these, a confusion of aromatic smells drifts across and suddenly I am ravenous. Soothing chants play in the background as we quietly stuff ourselves until neither of us can eat another thing. Swallowing my last mouthful, I am looking forward to another cool beer but Sean is up quickly, like last night, and already paying the bill. At the door he grabs a little packet of *paan* or spices and betel wrapped in a leaf and displayed on a tray. He pops the little package into his mouth and strides out. He seems agitated as he turns and says,"I'm sorry, Chloe, but I'm in a hurry. I have to get back to work on the bus again. We leave the day after tomorrow." And. spitting the leftovers of *paan* onto the sidewalk, he walks on, leaving the red splodge of betel juice on the asphalt.

"That's OK. You go on. I'm going to wander back

slowly," I call after his back as I dawdle along savouring everything about the evening.

"You sure you can manage?" Some way ahead he stops and calls out to me.

"Of course I can, Sean. I'm a grown up, middle-aged woman, remember?" My reply is confident with the optimism of the new and inexperienced traveller.

I wave at him as he strides off and into the night. "See you then," he calls over his shoulder.

Leaving the city high street, as I get nearer to the hostel I become aware of different movements around me. The 'night people' are silently arriving out of the shadows. Deciding to stay awhile and watch this unfolding scene I hide behind a tree, pulling my shawl over my head to cover my hair. First one figure then another unrolls a mat here, a blanket over there. I hear more chanting coming from behind some buildings to my right. Soon there are other sounds as fires of coals are made and lit and pots of ghee set to boil. The air becomes spicy and filled with sighs, or so it seems. The sigh of a weary body settling, a sigh of resignation and other sighs like the sigh when a hungry belly gets fed at last. That sigh almost one of contentment. Meagre possessions laid out along the roadside. A cooking pot. A small statue of Kali. A few wooden beads. And faces in the lamplight. Old faces. Resigned eyes. A rattling cough a few feet away and I quickly forget my hiding place to go to the curled form of an old woman who will probably not make another dawn. But beneath those thin tattered robes a heart still feebly beats for now. Saliva trickles from the corner of her mouth and her eyes are almost rolled up and into the sockets of her grey face. She is little more than a bag of bones. Someone has placed a cup of water beside her but her head only lolls as I try to help her and lift the cup to those cracked lips. It feels like I am lifting a tiny bird, a wren perhaps. Almost weightless. Only Heaven knows if joy ever lived here. I hope so for her sake because there sure can't be any joy right now. As I lay her head back down I am reminded of those tramps on the sidewalk in New York who got me into so much trouble as a child. *Dolores – are you still alive, I wonder? Did you ever get to see your child again?*

Another sound. A rising crescendo all around me of unintelligible murmuring. Unintelligible until I catch the words "Please, please". What starts as a whisper gathers momentum until I am engulfed by the repetitive sound as it washes over me and a rising tide of hands, so many hands, claw at the air and those nearest clutch at my clothes, begging for alms. An old man grabs at the hem of my shawl as more people come towards me. Oh my God! It's *me* they want! Stumbling and tripping, knocking over the old woman's water, I run on legs of cotton wool down the nearest dark alleyway, their pleading still in my ears but getting fainter the farther I run, until that other sound takes over. The chanting I had heard earlier is louder here and around the corner is a huge mosque, light flooding through the open doors and down the steps where a few white-robed people sit in small groups. Panting, my heart beating so painfully, stopping to lean back against the wall of a building held in the shadows, I can smell my body drowning in nervous perspiration. My Punjabi tunic is soaking and sweat trickles down my legs again. Sending up a silent prayer that no one will see me, I try to relax. *Breathe deeply, Chloe.* Then pounding feet coming in my direction. Too scared to look back, I start to move forward again but the feet come to a halt beside me.

"Madam, you leave your shawl."

My shawl! I put my hand to my head. Of course! I had felt a tug when it came off but in my panic I wouldn't stop. The young boy holding out my blue crinkly shawl can't be more than ten years old. Naked except for a pair of torn shorts, he wears the most engaging grin with a tooth missing in the middle. His face is streaked with dirt but his eyes are full of laughter.

"You dropped it, madam. And I picked it up." He says this so proudly. And he stands tall, thrusting his flat stomach towards me, his shoulders back.

Looking around to make sure no one sees, I reach for my purse and shakily give him some *baksheesh*. "But *please* don't tell your friends. Let it be our secret!" I beg as I put them into his small and grubby brown hands.

"Yes, madam. You very kind lady. I come with you?"

"Well… er… OK! You can escort me back to the hostel if you like." It will be a relief to have a companion.

Another gappy grin and he trots beside me as I put my shawl back over my head and tuck the tell-tale strands well away. Ahead is a sign, high on a building, for a post office. Not knowing quite what to do with it, I had stuffed the postcard I'd written to Jeannie in my pocket and I now draw it out. A soggier card than previously, but no doubt it will dry off before reaching the florists in New York!

We emerge from the eerie black alleyways and into a garishly lit area of bright lights and neon signs. Surprisingly, the post office is still open. My new friend waits outside as I go in and ask the khaki-sleeved man behind the counter for stamps. He looks at me with unexpected insolence and smirks when I ask where the post box is. As I drop the card through the slit of the metal box on the outside wall, I am instantly surrounded by a group of slight young men who boldly push me backwards with their hands. My little friend is nowhere to be seen. In a terrified moment I realise that I have seen no women on the streets this evening apart from the 'night people' huddled on the sidewalk.

"*Ouch!*" A pinch on the bum makes me jump. "What the hell are you doing?" My voice is just a squeak as a hand touches my damp breast and tweaks the nipple. "Please leave me alone!" But they pack tighter around me and back me up against the post office. Alcohol breath gusts all over my face as they rub their bodies up against me, grab at my breasts and laugh with open mouths and rotting teeth. There may only be five of them, but right now it feels like hundreds. A ludicrous flash of Spotty's assailant whistle pops into my mind and if I didn't feel so scared I would want to laugh. Anyway, the whistle is in my backpack at the hostel and I doubt if I could blow it even if I could get to it. This *has* to be Eve-teasing. So soon? It isn't a pleasant experience. I seem to be gasping for air. Rosie, you were right! I'm too old for all this!

"Beautiful blonde lady." And for the second time in an evening, my shawl is tugged from my sweat-sodden head.

"You English, American?"

"Beautiful lady!" A particularly revolting looking man with black front teeth lifts my tunic. "You want to fuck, lady?"

"I fuck you," says another. "You like it, madam."

"Fucking very nice. Me very good fuck!"

Must be the 'in' word! As they shriek with laughter and thrust their faces closer, they push their pricks against my body. Revulsion and bile, combining with the smell of their breath and unwashed bodies, rises up into my throat. I start to gag but it doesn't stop them. Those who can't get near enough seem to be rudely posturing and playing with themselves. Fucking postures!

Then, quicker than it takes to put this down on paper, fear flips over into rage and I find my voice at last. "I don't want fucking!" I shriek, lashing out with strength I didn't know I had. "In fact I wouldn't fuck you if you were the last man on earth!" This is aimed into the face of the blackened stumps as his fetid breath makes my head reel. He steps backwards as I spit in his face. Highly amused, they all fall about laughing and jeering at this unexpected retaliation.

"White ladies like fucking!" cries one man to another peal of drunken laughter as he waves his small but erect penis in my direction. "Fuck, fuck, fuck, lady!" he says in what he thinks is a tantalising sing-song voice. "You *love* it. It very nice."

It's when I go at the nearest man with my clenched fists that an unexpected thing happens. I clearly hear my name being called

"Chloe, what the hell d'you think you're doing?" Sean's arm comes out and grabs me. I choose this precise moment to throw up. Flecks of vomit spatter his silk shirt as, towering above the group, who fall apart giggling like naughty children, he now pushes me to his arm's length. "Ugh! How disgusting. Just what d'you think you're doing out at this time of night?" He looks ferocious and his tight grip bites into my arm. "How stupid can you be? Look around you. How many women do you see wandering these alleyways? Now march!"

I have barely finished heaving before he propels me around and we are going back in the general direction of the hostel. Raucous laughter following us. Still angry, I aim a sideways kick at his shins.

"How dare you speak to me like that! I told you earlier, I'm not a child but a middle-aged woman." And I try to shake his arm off.

"And a very stupid and naïve one, if I may say so," he hisses, but he does release his grip.

If I was looking for some sympathy I sure am not going to get it from this guy! With not another word spoken between us, we walk back to the hostel. Why doesn't he go away and just leave me alone? Anyway what was he doing out near the post office? Didn't I leave him earlier going in the opposite direction? I thought he was going to see to the bus. Didn't he say he had more repairs to do on it?

At the hostel gate he walks away without a backward glance but I notice a man stepping out of the shadows to join him and they disappear out of sight. I do feel stupid and, yes, naïve. I don't want to think about Sean or anyone else as I collapse onto my bed and lie there trembling. Fucking indeed! I always thought it a word without decent sentiment and now I know it's true. Now, 'wenching' carries a certain ring, as it juggles lust with laughter and mutual enjoyment. A bawdy confusion of doublet and hose, ribald laughter and rising petticoats. But it wasn't wenching on offer this evening, just an amusing fuck at the cost of someone else's discomfort. My discomfort, in this case. Well, if that's 'Eve-teasing', I can give it a miss. If anything my body feels as if it has detached itself and floated off somewhere more pleasant. It's kinda numb, I guess.

It isn't until the early hours that I sit up stiffly and remove my creased clothes. Falling back to sleep it is to dream of Spotty. "I warned you about Adam-teasing!"

It's with heavy shadowed eyes and a huge sense of lethargy that I get up to join the smart, air-conditioned coach that will take me on a tour of Old Delhi. But first I must shower, wash my hair, and rub soap vigorously all over my body to erase the story of last night. It is when I am pulling my tunic over my head that I realise it's gone. My butterfly! So I suppose you could say that it isn't only my eyes that feel heavy but my heart too. Losing the butterfly is a blow. Mike will always travel with me. I know that. He will always have a space in the home of my heart. It was just a bit of familiarity to hold on to, that's all. *Anyway, Chloe, for heaven's sakes, whoever said "Growing through Going" would be easy?*

Within moments Chandni Chowk casts her spell and transports me into another new world as we inch slowly along this narrow and congested open-air shopping bazaar. Rickshaws three deep and stretching into the far distance, Morris taxis, tourist buses jostling for space among the shops, stalls, colour and vibrancy. Colourful secondhand silk saris piled high and being picked over by tourists or buyers for foreign shops. The same saris to be revamped and transformed into trousers and shirts and resold in markets across the world. Crates with chickens, bubbling pots, goats, horses, sacred cows, spices of every kind. Something to capture the attention whichever way I look.

As we near the mosque I glimpse a line of beggars. But

the tour guide is quickly out first and clears a way through, telling us not to hang around, so that I don't really see anyone closely. Removing our shoes, we add them to the huge pile and then we hire long loose robes to wear on top of our clothes. Inside the huge courtyard is breathtaking and already some of the workmen are taking their siesta as they lie dead to the world, sprawled out across the steps. I almost envy them. My body aches, and just longs to sleep for a week to wipe out the memory of last night. So I won't climb the minaret but choose inertia instead, sitting in the shade to admire the architecture. Looking around me I see a familiar but unwelcome face entering the courtyard but almost immediately ducking down and into a small carved wooden door at one side of the entrance. Sean! What on earth is *he* doing here? And although I keep my eyes open I don't see him coming back out.

Down the steps again the tour guide is waiting to guide us back onto the bus. As he urges us to hurry to avoid the sudden crowding, the beggars who missed the first opportunity now surge towards us and I catch someone out of the corner of my eye. Someone different. Among the beggars, the bandaged lepers, the straggly file of the sick and deformed, is a man moving like a crab on all fours, his hands slipped into wooden sabots. Strong big man's hands, contrasting sharply with the tiny and hideously deformed child's feet. A naked man's body to the waist and a three-year-old child's from there on down, he moves slowly and painfully sideways as a crab does, his tiny bottom stuck up in the air above his heavily muscled chest and arms, his face and eyes never more than a few inches from the ground. Shepherded back to my window seat, I feel strangely disturbed by this human being who shares his view of the world with the insects that gather on the pile of dung lying just beside his nose. It quickly puts my own small world back into some kind of perspective.

"Please will you give that man, the one with the wooden sabots on his hands, this money?" Almost breathless, I hand a few rupees to the guide. "Make sure you give it to the right person, won't you?" Reluctantly, he gets off the bus but is back within a moment.

As the bus prepares to reverse and then starts its turnaround, I take one last look out of the window. In that same second it seems the crab man has moved and is now right below me, turning his head slowly and twisting it very stiffly sideways and then upwards. Our eyes find each other and lock together. In that split second, my world stops spinning and eternity ceases her endless journeying. Drowning in those liquid pools, my own eyes are surely mesmerised. And he *sees* me. No, I mean he *really* sees me. Like he sees right through all the layers, all those human veils I am wearing. On his beautiful face, black hair tumbling about it, is a look of love as he acknowledges me.

The moving bus jerks and pulls us apart and we start back along the busy street. Behind me, the crouched crablike figure on the ground grows smaller and smaller as I strain to hold him still among the crowd, not wanting to let the moment go. Not wanting to lose that feeling. A new and unfamiliar feeling that has come from a completely out of the ordinary gaze, throwing me off balance and making me suddenly aware that something deeply profound has just taken place.

"Please, who is that man?"

"Which man, lady?" The driver shakes my hand off.

"Please sit down, madam." The tour guide pushes me back into my seat.

"I need to get off. Please stop this bus."

"Madam. Please to sit down. You will cause an accident."

"That man. The one I asked you to give the money to. Who is he?"

"Just another beggar, madam." The guide is uninterested

"But he *can't* be. I mean…"

"There are many sick and deformed people here in India. Today you were lucky. Sometimes there are many more."

"Yes, but… I don't understand." I am not quite sure what I am trying to say. I can see he doesn't understand and I am not sure that I do either. I jump up again, feeling quite frantic, and move down the aisle to the front where the guide is now sitting opposite the driver. He turns towards me with an expression of badly concealed irritation and gets up. "Madam. I have to ask you again to sit down. You are disturbing this coach. Please to take the seat beside me." And he puts his arm behind my back and eases me into the seat beside him. How I can be disturbing a coach I cannot imagine, but I notice the lady with the pink rinse looking in my direction. The others are all looking out of the windows and into the crowded streets. I try one more time.

"Where does he live?" *How* does he live, so deformed that he could never sit down or do any of the normal things we take for granted?

"I told you, madam. He is just a freak from God and nature. It's even possible that his parents deliberately harmed him so that he could be this way. Then people like you will give him money. As to where he lives, I am not from this district, madam. I don't know exactly but somewhere here in Chadni Chowk, I expect."

Slumping back into my seat, I can't believe that no one else has noticed the Crab Man like I did. My mind goes over and over what I have just seen, confusion mingling with the knowledge that something extraordinary has just occurred.

A freak of nature or God? Does he mean a monster? A monster, no way. Of God?

I leave the question hanging. Over the next days I am to look at it from all the angles I know of. Words making no sense of this one deep look from a beautiful man.

But this was the moment the lotus bud began to blossom. In those few seconds the seed took root somewhere deep inside of me. Although I don't yet know it, my world has changed forever.

Chapter 5

The floaty Horizon trousers go into a carrier along with the thin, see-through sleeveless tops and the embarrassing swirly red skirt, and are left behind on my narrow bed. My three Punjabi suits are now my chosen way of dressing; being loose fitting with long sleeves, they are comfortable and modest. Make me feel less like a conspicuous giant and allow me to kid myself that I am blending in to my surroundings. What a mistake these newly blonde highlights were, the bleach making my hair dry and brittle under the sun. On an impulse, I discard my make up bag too, dropping it in the bin. War paint and lippy have no place here in this humidity. Besides, panda eyes don't suit me, so it's back to how I came into this world – the naked, soft and shiny red-faced look! And you know what? It feels more honest. Now I have nothing to hide behind! The face that stares back at me from the mirror has already gotten a different look about it; though I can't place it. Must be something to do with the Crab Man. Now, why did I think that? If only there was someone I could talk to about him. Even if she were here, Rosie would think I've truly gone mad and as for Jeannie... She would just laugh

at me. Suggest I must be sex-starved or something like that!
I'll just have to work it all out for myself. This desire to see
him again, to understand is, if anything, even more intense
today. Last night I couldn't sleep for thinking of him. The
image of his face constantly swimming before my eyes.

"Brett's such a ham, dear. Thinks he's having a breakdown.
He's just giving a performance, though *not* of a lifetime! Never
was much good as an actor anyway. Don't you bother about
him, darling."

My mother's no nonsense response to calls from Brett
make me smile. Why did I ever marry Brett? Trying to fill
that gaping hole inside of myself? He did make me laugh in
the beginning with all his theatrical stories and impressions
but his repertoire was limited and soon I knew it off by heart.
A doted-upon only child of elderly parents, he's remained
the indulged little boy looking for cookies and sulking when
he doesn't get them. I know he'll get over me quickly and
find another woman. Someone else to take care of his every
need, to be rewarded with a winning smile or another
anecdote. Another impersonation. I can picture him talking
to my mother on the phone, the pretended distress gathering
momentum the more he gets into the role of being my ex-
husband. He has dark, matinee idol good looks, boyish charm
and a winning way or, should I say, a way of winning – mostly
young ladies but not starring roles. I bet by the time I get
back he will have some minor starlet draped over his arm,
all big tits and not much else.

I had booked a time slot for the call box in the hostel
and, after speaking with my mother, I ring Bob to hear news
of Rosie. My two husbands. Brett and Bob. And yet neither

of them suited. But now, hearing that slow ponderous voice, I am glad all of a sudden that he's like he is, someone solid for Rosie.

"Take care, won't you, Chloe, and remember to stay in touch," he says as we ring off. Right now he's acting as a cornerstone for both of us.

"Yes, and thanks, Bob, for being who you are." *Who you are is conventional and sensible, uncomplicated and good.* Bob still wears the same crew-cut hair, grey now, the same clean cut boy-next-door looks. I can see our wedding photo – me barely out of high school and almost still in bobby socks. The long white satin dress, the blossoms in my hair, my hand clasping that of my new and acceptable husband, a look of hope in my eyes. Within a short space of time, the birth of Rosie brought new responsibilities and much joy as I gazed in wonder at the tiny bundled child. The small fist clutching at my finger, bringing with it those waves of tenderness and a fierce sense of protection. Her big eyes bright with trust. Her life depending on me. Have I been worthy of her trust, I wonder? My father's rantings when I left to live with Mike left me doubled up with guilt, doubtless his intended goal. Now, when I see that wide open and pretty face I know I didn't do too bad. At least we achieved a childhood full of love for her, Mike treating her like a much cherished and special friend, and Bob and I just adoring her. I am so glad she is exploring her wings. How different life might have been had I had the courage to step out of the mould much sooner. Stepped into my own world, casting aside someone else's plans for me and making my own.

A sharp tapping on the glass of the phone booth reminds me to stop my reverie and get moving. Gathering my things up I make way for the thin and freckly young girl waiting to make her call home.

By nine o'clock I am all packed and ready and making my way to the agreed meeting point along the road, keeping my eyes open for the guy, Jim, from Australia. Hitching my already much heavier bag into a more comfortable position, I wait by the trees alongside the avenue for the bus to arrive, the same avenue where I hid to watch the night people. Only now there are no beds on the pavement, no cooking pots or statues of Kali, no rasping coughs. Just a busy sidewalk full of tourists, mostly in their newly bought Indian clothes, just like me!

"Hello, lady. Look! I have your necklace!"

My gap-toothed friend! Or was he? He had simply vanished into thin air when I needed him. But now here he is, Mike's butterfly, with a broken chain, lying across his open palm. Must have been pulled off my neck the night before last. My heart gives one big giant leap and I want to kiss that dust-streaked little face with the gappy smile.

"Where *did* you find it? Thank you. Thank you." Life feels suddenly *so* good.

"It was lying on the ground outside the post office. I saved it for you."

"You certainly did! Thank you." If I didn't think he would be embarrassed I would hug that thin little body with the sticky-out ribs.

"Do you make a habit of this? Watching for things people drop?" First my shawl and now my necklace! Then a strange thought occurs to me. What if you made people lose things and then found them again for them? What if they were so delighted with you finding them that they gave you *baksheesh*? But how uncharitable a thought is that, Chloe? Yet again I reach into my purse and take out a little *baksheesh*.

"Over here, Chloe." Sean appears with a grim face and takes my backpack, his free hand under my elbow to steer me across the road. Looking back, I wave goodbye to Gappy whilst allowing myself to be lead to the other side. Is Sean still angry about the other night?

"Hey. Wait a moment. What about the others? Hadn't we better wait for them?"

"We'll be picking them up from their hotel in a moment. You get in and put your bag at the back." He doesn't look at me and seems distracted.

The old and ramshackle bus parked against the curb comes as a shock. I am sure it never looked like this in those brochures in East Grinstead! I try casting my mind back. Two windows are stuffed with cardboard, the paintwork is dull and scratched and there is a large dent on the side nearest to me. I am suddenly uncertain but my hesitation only lasts a second. After all, what difference does it make? We won't need windows, glass or board in this heat! Besides, I find Sean trustworthy, don't I? He did, after all, rescue me from those horrid guys outside the post office. He now makes an impatient, hurrying up gesture to me so I throw my bag in at the door, clamber up the step and choose the seat across the aisle from him, by the open doorway. Sean climbs on, starts the engine and we move forward and into the traffic without a word spoken. A little further along, outside a small and scruffy-looking hotel, he pulls up. "Put your foot on the brake pedal, will you?" And he gets out and goes inside. *What, the brakes don't work either?*

76

When he comes out he is alone. Moving across again as he climbs back on board, and keeping my foot on the pedal until he takes over, I can sense his tenseness. Putting the bus into gear he pulls out without a glance or word in my direction.

"Sean, *what* is going on here? I want you to stop the bus. *Now*! Please! A sense of alarm stirring inside of me. But this is ridiculous. There has to be some reasonable explanation. As I try not to give in to feelings of rising panic, Sean pays me no attention.

A mile or so on he parks off the road, switches the engine off and at last turns to look at me with a bored expression. "It's just you and me, baby! *Ugh! Please don't call me 'baby'.* "U Go Overland didn't get any takers. Simple as that."

"What do you mean, they didn't get any takers? Why would you drive all the way to Kathmandu with one passenger? It can't pay you to do that." Indignation gives way to the tiniest bit of anxiety again.

"Oh, that's simple. The bus can only remain in India for sixty days so it has to be moved out and I will be going to Kathmandu, anyway – with or without you." And he actually yawns, a 'take it or leave it' expression on his face.

"But why didn't you tell me? And what about the guy from Australia?"

"Listen, Chloe. U Go Overland is in the shit. The company is going down the pan. Your £800 will more than pay to get the bus up there. There was a guy coming from Australia but he cabled a few days ago to say he couldn't make it."

For a moment I don't know what to say, what to think. My brain feels like it is full of jumble. "But why didn't *you* tell me? I could have altered my plan. Now what am I going to do?"

Then he grins at me. "I guess we're stuck with each other. Better make the best of it, eh?"

I wonder why he doesn't smile more often. Mr Charming is back!

Four hours of driving in silence in sweltering heat and I'm bursting to pee. "I'm sorry, Sean, but I just have to pee."

He pulls over immediately and I climb out onto the desert like scrub that stretches forever.

"Stay close to the bus and watch out for cobras."

"Don't worry! After that piece of information, I'll glue myself to the bus." It's too hot to pull the shawl over my head so my hair really shows up among the squat bushes and the decorated lorry passes flashing and tooting its horn as the crew wave delightedly at "blondeee lady". The prickly dry grass tickles my bare bottom as I crouch, though I try to be discreet and drape my tunic over my knees.

It's another silent half-hour before we take a welcome break. The old-fashioned wooden handcart stands outside the coffee shop, one huge block of ice filling the whole of the open back. We pull up and Sean wedges a large stone under the front wheel of the bus because of the dodgy brakes.

"Hey! I thought you said you were mending the bus all this time!" I make it light-hearted but he doesn't hear me and guides me inside the darkened interior. Large mugs of iced coffee are put in front of us. He leans back and at last he looks me in the eyes.

"Look, Chloe. I'm sorry but the office just strung you along. This way, at least they get the trip paid. There's something else you should know too. I didn't want to do this trip. In fact I'm bored with doing this trip. I've done it so many times now. So I won't be stopping unless you ask me to. I just want to get there and get the hell out of it and back to England."

What can I say? That it wasn't only the office that strung me along, but Sean strung me along too? I thought about the nervousness of James in the office in Station Road and his obvious relief when I fell for his sales talk. Looking at Sean's petulant expression, I make the snap decision not to let him get to me. After all, he's right. If we are going to drive together, we should try to make the best of it. Besides, I would still get to Kathmandu. It just wasn't what I had expected, that's all. Wait till I tell Rosie.

"I thought we might pick up some other travellers. That way you'll have company – someone to talk to. We can charge them too. Divide the money between us." Is he trying to make me feel better? The way I'm feeling about U Go Overland at the moment makes cheating a bit feel OK. "If you see something you particularly want to photograph you'll have to shout and I'll stop. Is that understood?" And the way he says it makes arguing out of the question.

"Yes."

Rosie would probably shout at him. Demand her money back. But all I can think of is the Crab Man at the mosque and the way he lives his daily life. My hand finds the broken butterfly necklace in my pocket. I haven't come to India because of Sean but because of me. I want to see the country, travel across it, travel inside myself and grow within this new taste of freedom. Discover who I really am at last now that the leash is finally off. *Growing through Going*, remember?

What better way to traverse the Ganges Plains than by bus? Holding this thought, my decision is made in a second.

I would like to ask him what he was doing at the mosque in Chadni Chowk but decide this is not the moment, so I give a cool non-committal shrug. "OK. I think that all sounds just great." He shoots me a surprised look, one eyebrow quizzically raised.

How else was I going to get to know this country so well? Driving through it was already giving me a whole different perspective. Already I felt sorry for people who came and stayed in international hotels, took tourist air-conditioned buses and flew by plane from one big city to another. So that's how we came to move out and on.

Half an hour later, Sean warns me now to expect bogus road blocks – another unpleasant surprise. I am sure they never mentioned roadblocks. What do they mean? Almost as soon as the words are out of his mouth, we round a bend and have to slam on the brakes hard, skidding to a halt in front of a row of large rocks stretching across the width of the road. Immediately three skinny men approach Sean's side of the bus and demand money. One has a dirty bandage around his head and across one eye. With a shout to me to "Look out for the brake", Sean leaps out and as I make a swift move towards the brake, I watch as his temper erupts. Cursing loudly, he flings the rocks one by one away from the centre of the road, berating the now scared-looking trio who are retreating back to the road edge. With a thunderous face, he leaps back in and we roar away without a word spoken between us.

With a quick glance sideways at him, I decide I am right to trust him as far as my personal safety goes. What a complex man he is turning out to be.

Further on, we stop again but this time at a train crossing so we have time to buy samosas from the vendor squatting on the roadside, his karai of bubbling ghee beside him. The thin, crisp envelope is filled with the most succulent and delicious tasting vegetables. Sean turns then, giving me a wan grin. I give in!

"OK! I think you were great. Real Sir Galahad! Thanks."

We concentrate on eating. As the train passes and the pole rises, we lick our fingers and away we go again. The next roadblock is a police one but without boulders across the road. Just a sort of sentry box with several policemen waving at us to halt. Sean yells at me to hold on as he roars past them without stopping and keeps his foot down until well on down the road. Although I keep looking anxiously behind me no sirens follow us and we settle back. What was all that about?

"Relax, sweetheart!"

Sweetheart? Another new departure and one I won't think about. He offers me a *beedi,* that slim brand of Indian cigarette tied with a piece of thread at one end. Although I accept, it doesn't do much for me. Too much khendu leaf and not enough tobacco for my taste. I want to ask what the police wanted but don't want to break what almost seems a comfortable silence.

Along the road to Jaipur we stop and pick up Judith and Wolfgang, who are hitching. Judith, small and dark, from Israel, hitched up with Wolfgang only two days ago. She is as dark as he is blond. They are travelling on together. After throwing their bags in the back they quietly settle into the dirty seats behind me.

We move on again and pass into the 'Pink City'. The central street is wide and impossibly congested but once we turn off we are on a narrow rough dirt track where cows rummage in the garbage piled in the open sewers and pigs eat shit and sleep in the overflowing gutters. Camel carts, buffalo, the smell of bodies and spices. Colourful people and children are everywhere I look. Whichever way I turn, there is another picture, another story to absorb. I just can't wait to get out.

The bus turns into the weed-strewn drive of a small faded hotel. I discover that the loos don't work, rats run around outside my door and monkeys play chattering on the roof but the rich tapestry catches me up in its threads and so these details are of no importance. I put a bucket over the drain hole, step among the rats and avoid the cockroaches that seem keen to skid across the floor in front of me.

Sean can't be persuaded to come and eat, so the three of us go into the main street, find a comfortable curry house and get to know each other better over food. When it gets dark we wander lazily back, chattering easily, bright stars overhead.

It's when I close my door that I see the note. *I won't be here tomorrow but Bhaskar will look after you.* Who the hell is Bhaskar? And what is going on now? Oh well! Only one way to find out. Wait and see. The monkeys on the roof sound as if they are playing a football match but at last sleep comes along with the thought "Who are we really, these strange creatures called human beings?"

If I was hoping for an answer in my dreams, I am disappointed but I seem to remember the Crab Man's face looking into mine just before I fall to sleep, and awakening in the morning refreshed and with a feeling of contentment.

Judith is 19 and will be returning to University in Tel Aviv. Her family live on a kibbutz near Qumran in the desert, almost opposite Jordan and quite near to where the first Dead Sea scroll was found in a cave. From Judith's home you can see the cave high up above them. The kibbutz has a date farm and I listen fascinated to how they all live in a community. They have a tiny zoo of animals for the children, and a shop and laundry and tennis courts. A whole world contained behind a barbed wire fence and guarded by soldiers with shotguns. A vulnerable world, it seems to me.

Tall Wolfgang, on the other hand, is 24 and has just finished his degree in economics. He comes from Dusseldorf and lives in an apartment shared with other students. His world is more free, less fearful. These two young people remind me of Rosie and her friends, something to do with the way they are so at ease with one another, even though they have only just met.

Just as we are finishing our breakfast together, a slender young man wearing a peacock brocade waistcoat over his otherwise naked torso wanders languidly over and introduces himself as Bhaskar. He is very beautiful, with an aquiline nose set between deeply fringed eyes. Like a cat, with his tanned and lithe body almost liquid in its feline way of moving.

A short climb later and we are in a deserted spot high above the city, where Bhaskar introduces us to the impressive marble cenotaphs of the Royal Family, each one intricately carved. Each month the inhabitants of the village below lay flowers here. Before we were allowed up to this area Bhaskar bought sweets as a bribe to the village headman, which he now hands over. "So you will be untroubled on your journey through his village."

"Yes, but why boiled sweets?"

"He has a sweet tooth," Bhaskar grins.

"Do you mind if I ask you something, Bhaskar?"

"No, madam. Please to ask."

"How well do you know Sean?"

He looks uncomfortable and avoids my eyes all together as he looks down and scuffs the ground with his bare brown toes.

"Not long, madam," and he moves abruptly away from my side to join the others in front.

Walking back down the hill again we pass yards of sari fabric, freshly dyed and left lying on the ground to dry outside a small wooden house. Magenta, orange and deep turquoise. Rich vibrant rivers cascading across the grey baked earth. And on past the local laundry, the *dhobi ghat*, where piles of clothes are washed, scrubbed and pounded in the grey river water, by the *dhobi wallahs*. Clothes waiting to be washed in colour assorted piles lying all around. In another area clothes lie out to dry in rows and strung across the roadside hedges are tee-shirts and knickers of all shapes and sizes. From big cotton bloomers to dainty and lacy and not a thong in sight. Wearing no knickers is preferable to wearing those. The plain white cotton briefs I have on now were bought from a roadside stall.

"That's the ironing shed over there." Bhaskar points to a shed behind the *ghat*. Which scene reminds me that I really need to get my clothes washed and he promises to send a boy to collect my dirty washing. He then leaves us to have the afternoon to ourselves so I wander along the streets with

Judith and Wolfgang. Over sweet mint tea Judith asks me, "How well do you know Sean, Chloe?"

"Not very well at all, why?"

"His behaviour is a bit strange, isn't it?"

"I think he's just moody that's all. Bored with doing this trip." And we leave it at that.

"Imra, what a beautiful name!" I tell the gorgeous child who comes to collect my washing. His deep walnut eyes are patient as I collect my clothes together and wrap them into a bundle in yesterday's Punjabi suit. "Does it have a special meaning, the name Imra?"

"Yes. It means a fable." And he shyly bows his head as I hand him my bundle. "I bring it back tomorrow morning, madam."

"So soon? That's great. Bye now."

Little Fable scampers off through the back gates and out onto the pitted street with the open running sewers and the squealing pigs, my washing clutched to his chest. Tomorrow I shall give 'the beautiful fable' Imra the rest of my clothes.

A knock on my door wakes me and I see from my watch that it is already eight o'clock. Pulling a shawl over my new sarong, I open it to find Mr Charming, grinning from ear to ear. "Morning, Chloe. Sorry about yesterday. Hope Bhaskar was helpful. Breakfast?" He doesn't wait for answers. Is this guy trying to be masterful or what?

"Hey, hang on. I haven't got any clothes on. I have to get dressed first."

"No problem. I'll wait inside, shall I?" And with another broad grin he steps into my bedroom.

"If you must, but it means I'll have to change in the shower then." I pull a face at him as I gather up my clothes and go into the pretence of a shower room. Not the easiest place to get dressed in, nor the most salubrious or fragrant. Overnight the upturned bucket I placed over the drain has shifted, but no sign of a rat.

"Anyway, what's got into you? How come you're so bright and cheerful today?" I shout at him through the closed door as I struggle to pull the tunic over my head. His sunny mood makes it easy to respond. Besides, I feel like I'm flirting! It's so long since I did I can't be certain but it's stirring a chord somewhere.

"Nothing. Just had a day off, that's all. Like I told you, I've been to the cenotaph hundreds of times. And no doubt you stopped to look at the laundry too, *and* the sari workshop?" And he gives a mock yawn of boredom.

"I won't ask how you guessed. Where were you yesterday?" I might as well take advantage of this ebullience.

"That's for me to know and you to guess!" is his playful retort as he ruffles my hair when I pass him to scoop my shawl from the bed. "I had some business to see to," he adds in that final way people say things when they don't want any questions asked. End of that conversation.

There is a neat pile of my washed and ironed clothes just outside the door with a little note, like a bill, on top. A list of my clothes sent for washing written in childish grey pencil: *1 Punjabi, 3 underneath* [I think he means knickers], *1 tunic!*

Soon, I am swung in the air in an act of collaboration between the elephant, the red turbaned wallah and me, my *Lonely Planet* guide having wetted my imagination and making this one place I really didn't want to miss visiting. I risk Sean's mood swings and persuade him to take us to the Amber Palace and Fort, eleven miles out of Jaipur and situated on top of another hill. While he refuses to walk up to the palace, preferring to stay below and chat with the elephant wallahs, the three of us sit atop an exotic tasselled *howdah* on this huge elephant with the strangely painted face, red fabric tumbling down her sides.

"Don't spend too long up there," Sean mutters after us as we start to lumber slowly up the hill. But this beautiful creature isn't in any hurry as she so carefully places one huge foot in front of the other. Perched on top, queen of all I see from my exotic canopied seat, I am swayed into a daydream until, minutes later, we reach a courtyard in this elaborate and intricately ornate palace fort, once the capital of Jaipur with its silver, gold, and jewelled inlaid rooms, now empty of furniture but magnificent in architecture and work-manship. The elephant – I never do discover her name – bends her knee and, swinging one leg over the other, I slide down towards it until I feel the crinkly hide, like sandpaper, underneath my left foot. The wallah takes my hand as I step down. Looking into the elephant's small eye, I think I detect a gleam of amusement as she puts out her trunk and gently messes my hair. (That's twice in one day!) When I pat her, she flaps her ears at me very, very slowly.

Way down from the ramparts, Sean is a distant speck deep in conversation. I wave but he doesn't turn. Instead, he and the other men pass under the archway and disappear from sight. It's so easy to lose all sense of time up here, wandering through the various mirrored halls and royal apartments. I know that the women spent most of their time inside these fortified walls while their men fought the battles. My mind conjures up the swordsmen in the narrow passageways and, looking over the ramparts, I picture the tented city there might have been down below. How must it feel to be a woman incarcerated so high up in such a place of perfumes and mirrored beauty? Temples, gardens, frescoed ceilings and silver doors. Pillared pavilions, palaces and gateways to be wandered through. The intricate pieces of inlaid silver mirrors reflecting the sun, tumbling fountains and the flower-laden air aid my trip down an imagined memory lane as I sit in the shade of a tree. 'Safe' is a word that comes to mind. Like a child might feel in its mother's arms. Like the safe camp I used to make for Rosie under the kitchen table. Together, we would fetch comforters and rugs and put them over the tabletop until they touched the floor all around it. Inside we put cushions and then we would sit and take tea out of tiny cups, eat pretend cookies, safe from the big bad giant outside! But incarcerated in the *zenana*, the women's apartments, I might have felt trapped among all this perfumed splendour. My childhood convent days come to mind. No, I would definitely long to break out and join the men fighting under a free sky.

Thinking about Rosie brings a sudden pang and a desire to see those clear eyes, that lovely youthful face. I wish she were here to share the joy of watching each new discovery revealing itself in all its seductive beauty. Rosie combines the very best of me and Bob. She has his thoughtfulness, his steadiness but not seriousness, and my constantly enquiring mind and the sense of humour I lost somewhere along the way. *No, be truthful Chloe. You lost it after Mike. He took my laughter with him when he died.*

Sean's shout breaks the memories. I think he's mouthing "Have you finished? We need to get back." Sighing and calling out to the others, I make my way outside through the intricate Mughal garden, past the steps leading to the small Kali Temple, the Goddess Kali being the Goddess of Death and Destruction, prayed to for victory during battles. I am becoming fascinated with all these different deities and should try to find a book. I must ask Judith if she has seen any bookstores.

We walk across to a waiting jeep and regretfully we are driven away from this exotic palace and back down to the bus where Sean is looking petulant again and the drive back is made in silence.

"There you are. I thought I heard a voice from home!" A very ample and blue-rinsed lady, perspiring freely, bears down upon me from across the restaurant, her long, orange kaftan billowing out around her huge bulk and a shawl of shades of purple thrown across her shoulders. "I'm Edna. Edna from Louisiana!" And she sticks out a heavily ringed hand with lilac nails.

"Oh, er, I'm Chloe. I'm from New York, actually."

Her round face beams and her second chin wobbles A pity really, because she has nice eyes and very smooth skin if it weren't for the little flakes of pink powder sticking to it.

"Is this your first trip, Miss Chloe?" And without waiting for a reply: "Of course, I used to live here. Forty-five years ago for ten years. May I?" she drawls, indicating the vacant seat. Judith's face is a picture. Edna pauses for effect for a split second and eases her great bulk into the chair. Really, her timing is perfect. "I came on a vacation and didn't go home." Then, leaning forward conspiratorially, "He was *gorgeous*!" And she giggles gloriously like you imagine a hyena might. "Of course, I never could resist a dark skin," she leans forward to whisper loudly in my ear, massive cleavage bobbing just below my eyes. "There's nothing quite like it, you know." A stifled cough from Sean as he reaches for more water. Edna picks up a paper napkin and fans herself. "I promised I would come back someday and now here I am."

"I'll leave you two to talk." Suddenly Sean is on his feet and making his way out. Pausing only to chew some cardamom seeds, he leaves some money on the counter. Right at this moment I could cheerfully murder him! The rat! I could just get up and go to my room, of course, but it would look rude. Maybe I'll wait a bit and let the old gal talk! Great Aunt Lil comes to mind – must be something to do with the spirit of the woman. She must be in her seventies at least.

"Nice looking man, your fella."

"My fella? He's not my fella!" The very idea of it! "Oh no! I'm just travelling in a bus with him."

"Good for you, honey. A ring on the finger makes no difference at all. It's all in the chemistry." She can't have heard me. "Oh my! Is that the time?" she cries as she peers at her watch.

"I shall have to be goin' along now or I'll be late for my massage. See you later, Miss Chloe." Almost skittishly, she pulls herself up and out of her chair and whirls away out of the door. Now I remember seeing the handwritten notice for massage pinned up behind the reception desk. My mind boggles at the picture.

Sean reappears as if by magic. "Sorry to leave you like

that. I just wasn't in the mood for the old bat. I hid around the corner until I saw her go. I'll walk you back." And he does.

But later, when I leave my room to get fresh water, I see him leaving on the back of a motorcycle. A flash of the driver's peacock brocade waistcoat catches in the lamplight as they pass through the gate.

Chapter 6

Sean opts out, of course, and so have the young lovebirds, but this I couldn't miss. Like an exotic jewel box sprinkled with amethysts from Persia and corals from Arabia, garnets, agates and onyx all fashioned into beautiful, colourful patterns, the memorial 'the world will never forget'. Watching from a bend in the Yamuna River, as the first silent rays of the dawn sun catch the Taj Mahal, transforming her marble beauty from pink to gold, inspiration over centuries, for poets, musicians, writers and surely lovers. The boy's laughter from the river behind breaking the silence and carried on the warm air. Before me, a heartbroken Shajahan's memorial to his beloved wife Mumtaz. His word made flesh. As the smell of the frangipani flowers, laid fresh every day, mingle their perfume with the sensuous sandalwood incense, I stand in front of Mumtaz's tomb and am swept away into their great love story. Although I know the real tomb is underneath, because my guidebook tells me so, the air is heavy with their love – or so it feels to me. With a red rice bhindi placed on my forehead comes a moment of extraordinary anticipation, every nerve in my body tensing as if waiting for something to happen. As his picture swims in front of my eyes, I see him standing right there in front of me. No, not Mike, not Shajahan but the Crab Man. Those deep and luminous eyes boring into mine as I slip away into some other space.

"She's fainted. Please to stand back!" These are the last words I hear until "She's coming around now" and hands are stroking my temples and a strong smell hits my nostrils. Underneath me the floor is cool and I can see lots of feet, some bare, some with rings on painted toes, others dainty, in embroidered slippers and some in dirty plimsolls with holes where dirty toenails poke out. They are all around me and I realise the smell is a mixture of thick flowery perfumes and smelly feet! Someone helps me to sit up and I lean for a moment, still dizzy, against the tomb of Mumtaz. "Come, lady, drink this water. Then you must come outside and we make you some tea." The old lady's dark eyes are kind as she gabbles at the others to move out of the way and let me through, her green and gold sari rustling, as she walks slowly beside me, one hand under my elbow. In the square office near the entrance, she sits me down and goes away for a moment. There is a picture of Ganesh, the Elephant God, hanging on the otherwise bare wall. The mint tea when it comes is thick and very sweet but it does the trick. My head finally stops swimming and I am back in the present. Strangely, nothing hurts although now she probes the back of my head with gentle fingers and finds a sore spot. An ice cube wrapped inside a cloth is quickly applied. The freezing ice burns away any small bump I might have.

"No, really I'm fine now! I'm so sorry. I can't think what happened!" Should I tell her about the Crab Man? That inside of me the lotus bud has loosened a little bit more.

That for a split second my heart moved. That just as I reached the ground I felt its lurch. And now it doesn't seem to hurt a bit. But I felt it move. Not the flip it did for Mike. A different kind of flip. It doesn't feel bad and I don't feel afraid, but I *have* to go back to Delhi. So many questions to ask. I have a ticket for Calcutta in ten days' time but after that I will go back. What was it my mother had said? "Always so impetuous, Chloe." I looked the word up in a dictionary of synonyms once: 'fiercely ardent'. Well, that's how I feel. Fiercely ardent, burning almost, with desire to see him again. I thank her and go to sit on a seat in the shade as she waves me goodbye. Her glass bangles catch in the sun's rays as she raises a hand in salutation and, putting her palms together, inclines her head. "*Namaste.*"

I would have stayed for hours just sitting peacefully in the gardens but I am politely asked to move on as others begin to arrive with the hotter morning sun. The spell broken, reluctantly I move away. I am told the line of beggars here is huge and soon they will be gathering outside the gates and, besides, Hari Harsh is waiting for me. Last night when we arrived here in Agra he was waiting to greet Sean. Hari, not a great sight, with his unwashed appearance and bottle of booze in one hand, but they greeted each other like old friends. After a hassled night, spent mostly awake, as one man after another pounded on my padlocked door in the dreary hotel, it felt like I had only just fallen asleep before it was time to get up. My voice is hoarse from shouting "Go away!"

"Please to come out, madam!"

"No, I won't. Go away!"

And I put a chair under the door handle to make quite sure I was safe from unwanted intruders.)

Hari had offered to take me in his rickshaw at dawn break to the Taj and Sean insists that I can trust him. Now, sure enough, he is waiting just outside the gates. As the first leper, his right leg a bandaged stump, limps forward, crutch under his armpit, Hari leads me quickly away to the rickshaw, a stale smell of alcohol accompanying us. We make an unscheduled stop along the way at his brother's mosaic sweatshop, where little children are sitting on a dirt floor fitting small and intricate pieces of mosaic into low round table tops. They seem happy enough as they grin and show off their handiwork in this dark shed. I am feeling embarrassed because, much as I would like to, I just can't carry tables around India with me. A disappointing customer, I only buy a small blue papier mache elephant which, whenever I look at it today, takes me back to those smiling faces and the memory of that dawn visit to the Taj.

Further along the road, Hari jumps out and is on his knees in the dust down beside me. *Oh no! For heavens sakes! Please! Not another marriage proposal!*

"Please to take me with you! I beg you! I will be your slave! I will do anything you say. You can beat me. Do with me whatever you wish! Only please to take me with you!!" A slave proposal! And you know what? It feels uncomfortable and not a bit funny. (Sorry, Hari, no can do!). And I really *am* sorry when I see the dejected way his whole body droops in response to my rejection. Now he climbs back in and it's in silence that we make our way.

Back at the hotel I can't quite believe my eyes as the sight of Edna heaving her bulk out of a tourist taxi fills me with a sense of disbelief. A nightmare vision of coral chiffon with a large straw hat trailing a puce scarf, the colours screaming at each other and her naturally florid complexion. I had last said goodbye to her in Jaipur.

"Chloe, honey, I am just *soooo* thrilled at the thought of travelling alongside of you all!" Her long southern drawl seems even more pronounced today.

What! Just for a moment I am completely stunned and caught off guard. This trip is becoming madder and more bizarre by the moment!

"I must speak to you, honey! You'll never guess who I saw last night!" And she blushes, the red growing right up her neck and flushing her already perspiring face. Sean appears down the hotel steps and goes to help her take her bags across to the bus. Hari has another swig out of his bottle. Over Sean's head, Edna winks at me, her purple eye shadow smudged among the pouches of flesh beneath her eyes. Judith and Wolfgang now arrive, hand in hand, sleepy-eyed after a night of lovemaking, I imagine. They have obviously been warned, for they greet Edna easily and climb onto the bus. Still speechless, I collect my bag and follow them on. "What's going on *now*, Sean?" My whisper goes unanswered.

"More coming! We may have to wait a few minutes." Deliberately avoiding my eyes it seems, he sits back in the driver's seat. He's back in his shorts and grubby singlet today, although I did get a whiff of freshly soaped body as he pushed past me. Five minutes later Beth and Guy, a brother and sister from Scotland, roll up together with another young couple, William and Phoebe. They all pile on and we move off. All four of them, I find out later, are in their gap year between school and university. As he passes Sean, I notice William hands him some money. They all seem to have such small backpacks compared with mine, which feels heavier every time I pick it up.

Choosing the seat to the side, right up front and near the open bus door, I settle myself. Edna is undecided but finally plumps down across the back seat, spreads her skirts over her huge knees and fans herself with her straw hat.

Sean turns towards me with a wicked grin. "Remind me to take a group photo sometime!" I can't help laughing with him though I do feel a bit cross, as I remember that other group photo shown to me by James in the office in East Grinstead with that 'lively old man Mr Hodge!'

Sean is suddenly acting like a tour guide in spite of his earlier protestations when we left Delhi. Could this be something to do with the money he has been taking and which so far I have seen nothing of? Inside the Red Fort surrounded by its massive walls and its ten metre wide moat, my eyes are drawn towards the Octagonal Tower, yet another monument that Shajahan built for Mumtaz. It was here, with its views of the River Yamuna and the Taj, that he died, a prisoner of his son, his monument to his beloved always in his sight. Within this 'city within a city' we go on to visit the Pearl Mosque and the Hall of Public Audiences, and eventually pass outside the walls through a throng of beggars, mutilated children and lepers, a very bored looking Sean now guiding us through, before taking the road towards Kajuraho. Garish, brightly-decorated lorries with instructive signs on the back ('Hoot Before Passing!') and buses, their passengers overflowing onto the roof, dancing bears with rings through their noses, Sacred Cows and goats all add to the colourful travelling circus weaving its erratic way along these roads. I sit back and think about the Crab Man. What strange phenomenon is this? Oddly, I feel more curious than concerned.

The magic of that dawn is followed by a magical night to remember among the soaring ruins and temples of Orcha, where cows wander in and out of the deserted, frescoed buildings. My simple tiny room high up in the jungle has a stone slab for a bed, whitewashed walls and a stunning view. Falling asleep amongst the stars, I hear the crickets singing and the bray of a donkey. "If there be a paradise on earth, it is this, it is this, it is this." What a perfect day. My eyelids close. His face comes.

Crossing vast fertile plains and wide rivers next day, we reach the home of the erotic temples as dusk gathers. Khajuraho. Our stopping place here for the night has either dormitory or basic accommodation. While I prefer the basic, as do Edna and Sean, the six young ones go for the windowless dormitory with its rows of beds. All of them behave as if they have known each other for years and have been chatting away throughout the drive. Swapping places they have already visited and giving tips. By now I am carrying my own Indian tablecloth, bought from a street stall, which, pulled up under my chin, serves as my sheet or sarong so grubby beds no longer bother me. But basic also means a fan of sorts and sure enough, an old wooden fan slowly rotates in this room with its peeling walls, dripping taps, basin without a plug and the usual quota of cockroaches. There is also the sweetest small lizard darting about the walls.

After checking in and a quick wash, we meet together in the small town. Sean arrives late, as we are already halfway through our vegetable thali laced with the now expected copious amounts of cumin. I am practising eating with my fingers, pushing the food into the chapatti envelope held in my hand, and feel a bit like a messy child with greasy fingers to lick and a faceful of curry. When Sean pulls out a chair opposite me, he leans back in the seat.

"Chloe, I don't feel too good, I'm sorry. I've got the gut ache." Well, he does look rather green and soon gets up and leaves us. Edna too has stayed behind to rest. "Remind me to speak to you later, honey," she says in a loud and penetrating whisper, before I leave to come downtown.

Going back to my room I stop and knock on Sean's door. Bhaskar opens it and is as surprised to see me as I am to see him

"Oh, I'm sorry, I just wanted to ask Sean how he was feeling."

"*Namaste.* Not too good but will be better tomorrow, please to God." And he retreats back inside, closing the door quickly but not so quickly that I don't get a glimpse of a dishevelled bed and a prone figure.

Yes, please God indeed. How did *he* get here? I am just cleaning my teeth when there is another knock and there is Edna, resplendent in a lime kimono of rambling black dragons. A green scarf wrapped around her head. Long gold earrings dangle from her ears and her arms are now covered in cheap but bright and shining Indian bangles in greens and blues to match. Is this her night attire? She is carrying something in her hands. I can't see what it is because it's covered in what looks like a square of bright green silk.

"Am I too late, honey?" She pushes past me and into the room. She plops heavily onto the bed, kicks her gold mules off, places the silk square with whatever is underneath it beside her and lies back for a moment, her eyes closed, before sitting suddenly bolt upright, chins quivering

"I just *have* to share this with you. You'll never guess who visited me last night." A dramatic pause is left hanging.

"I can't imagine, Edna. Do tell me," I say, trying to sound enthusiastic.

"Clark Gable." This is said with such a triumphant flourish that my look of astonishment passes unnoticed.

"Yeah, I was just in the tub when he came in. He brought me such a nice bouquet. Roses! Red ones! Real pleased to see me, he was. Can you believe it, honey?" And she closes her eyes.

Clark Gable! Hasn't he been dead for years? Is she *on* something?

"*Such* a lovely man," she says wistfully as two tears squeeze out of her shadowed eyes and make a slow journey down the furrows of her over-powdered and already damp cheeks. "Of course I knew him really well, you know." She is suddenly silent.

"Er, um, does he often visit?" I find I am lost for words.

"Oh yes. Him and the others, of course." (What! *more* of them?) And suddenly noticing my expression, she adds, "Oh, didn't you know, can't you tell? I'm psychic, you know!"

The penny drops! I really want to giggle but don't want to hurt the feelings of this apparently quite crazy but lovable old girl.

"I brought my crystal ball with me. Thought we might

have a little peep just for you! See what your young man is up to." And with these words she whisks the green silk off the round glass ball in a single sweeping movement. Taking it in her hands, she focuses upon it with wide eyes. "Oh, dear! How upsetting! Very disappointing. I'm sorry but this is not what I expected at all and I don't like the look of it." She quickly retrieves the green silk and covers the glass ball, her lips pursed.

Intrigued now in spite of myself, I let myself be drawn in. "What is it? What have you seen?"

"Now don't you worry yourself, Miss Chloe. I'm not quite myself tonight. Don't always read it right."

"Oh, do tell!" I make my way across and sit down beside her on the bed. The crystal ball twinkles between us.

She pats my knee. "Now don't you go worrying yourself on account of me. We"ll try again another night." And she heaves herself up and makes her way, a little unsteadily, across the floor to the door. Just before leaving she turns and, before I know what's happening, hugs me and for a second I am caught in those fleshy folds smelling of damp lavender. "Those green Irish eyes can't always be trusted, you know. Sweet dreams, Miss Chloe." As she passes me to leave my room, she adds, "Of course, that Scarlett O'Hara led him such a dance."

Now I am completely confused! It's ages before I can settle because I keep giggling, seeing Clark Gable talking to a naked Edna in the tub! I am sure I fall asleep laughing. My dreams are all jumbled up with Edna and Sean and the Crab Man living together in a house called Tara. There is still a smile about me when I wake next morning.

A message comes via Bhaskar telling us all to do our own thing and visit the temples. Sean is better, will be spending the day in bed but will meet us this evening.

As you would expect, the erotic temples are exactly that. Even athletic looking Wolfgang and petite Judith have to laugh at some of the more extreme sexual positions of these meandering sensual sculptures. A memory of that night when Mike and I studied the Kamasutra together, wishing to explore the Tantric tradition of union between the divine and the physical. Setting the scene with flickering candles, incense burning and seductive Indian music. With the illustrations of the intricate positions open on the table beside the bed, we attempted to create even greater magic moments with this erotic 'art of lovemaking manual' beside us. After a complicated half hour of advanced gymnastics, closing the book and, collapsing into laughter, settling for our familiar and most favoured positions. Now, watching the quick glance exchanged between this young couple, I can't help a secret smile to myself. I wonder what they are thinking. Are they at ease with each other's bodies? That phase of exploring intimacy?

The three of us wander on among these remaining lofty temples dedicated to the various Hindu Gods. All twenty two of them, like a row of small hills, or tent rocks of New Mexico, climbing up to touch the peak of the Sikhara. Of course, my imagination is fired by the legend of Hemavati, the beautiful widow who gave herself to the Moon God when he, dazzled by her beauty, came down to earth. The child of that union was the founder of the Chandella Dynasty and creator of these erotic Tantric Temples whose exotic and decorative details express all the various stages of rapture.

I find all the different moods of love are here in all her various forms. I touch the butterfly in my pocket and for a second the face of the Crab Man swims into my vision again. I am surprised and confused that it isn't Mike's face.

"Are you all right, Chloe?" Judith's query brings me back into the present but now I bring an unused-to feeling of serenity with me.

There are more temples in another part of the village so I have a short walk, then take a rickshaw. Although I am certainly no Hemavati, I 'dazzle' the 16-year-old boy, acting as guide, who grabs me into his arms and presses his lips to mine in a touch of the "Please will you marry me and take me with you?" syndrome. Looking at all that sexual expression everyday must make him believe he too has the power or attraction of a Moon God! We are in a pedal rickshaw when he courageously pulls down the hood and lunges at me with his hot curry breath. Sure is good for the morale, all these proposals!

"No, please! I'm old enough to be your mother!" I plead as, disentangling myself, I try to keep it all in good humour. Besides, its too hot for clinches! The front of my Punjabi suit is now soaked. So we put the hood back up again and continue on our way and the driver just keeps pedalling on. I can hardly bear to look at the old man's straining shoulders as he cycles up a slight incline. In fact I think I need to get out and walk. I will never get used to travelling in this way on a human packhorse.

So I ask him to stop and walk back slowly to the hotel stopping to buy cards to send to my mother and Rosie. It's little more than a wooden kiosk but it is stacked up from floor to ceiling. Bars of soap and toilet paper sit beside a

crate of apples, exercise books, biros and cans of Fanta. The owner sits on a stool in the corner, the only space left, and from there he reaches down, leans over or turns behind him, everything being within arm's reach. The cards are old and faded and one has a slight stain across one corner but no matter.

Again that evening Sean doesn't appear but sends a message. The rest of us walk into the village and sit outside a café, passing on the way a muddy pool with a few reclining buffalo keeping cool, watched over by a small boy. Almost indistinguishable from the grey water they lie in, only their eyes move as we pass by. Sensual, colourful women, bare midriffs, arms and ankles covered with bells and bracelets and wearing sparkling bhindis between the eyes, wave at us as they wash the steel cooking pots outside their modest homes. We must look like a funny cosmopolitan lot with a panting Edna in yellow bringing up the rear. Another kaftan today, worn with an enormous necklace of big wooden beads and a bracelet to match.

Almost as soon as we are seated, a huge commotion breaks out. A cobra has been seen sliding beneath our table! Edna squeals, "Oh, my!" as men, armed with sticks and shouting at each other, bang the ground. Everyone talks at once and no one listens to anyone. By now we are standing on our chairs, though Edna remains seated, simply lifting her legs up to display inches of large puce bloomers and rolls of flesh. Of course the cobra takes off. But *where to* exactly? No one seems to know. All so busy shouting and making a noise, they forget to watch him. We finish our meal with a certain frisson of impending danger in the air. In

a room upstairs, someone is singing and the sound falls gently down upon us. The wax flowers of the frangipani hang above us, showering us with their perfume.

Later, returning to the hostel by moonlight, I notice for the first time the armed soldier standing outside the hostel gate. I wonder what that's all about. Perhaps Bhaskar will know; I must ask him.

Undressing and winding myself into my tablecloth, I sit under the fan at the bottom of the hard bed and start to write postcards, one to my mother and another to Rosie, care of Bob. Heaven alone knows when she will get it! What a lot we are going to have to talk about when we see each other again! Looking at the photo of her gorgeous face, I kiss it gently before tucking it under my pillow. I do this every night. Feel it connects us somehow, helps to keep each other safe.

When the knock comes I am sure it must be Edna with news of more nocturnal visitors, but it is Bhaskar standing there to tell me that we leave tomorrow morning as planned.

"Sean must be better then?"

"Yes. Feeling much better."

He doesn't linger, lunge, propose marriage or voluntary slavery, so another ten minutes and I am in bed and getting lost with the Crab Man again.

Next morning Sean is grey-faced but with a curt nod at us all he gets into the driver's seat and we set off in the direction of Varanasi. No sign of Bhaskar! I am in my seat by the open door and Edna in the back again, well spread out, a book of astrological signs beside her. No doubt checking her stars to see if they are compatible with Clark Gable's!

Phoebe lying with her head in William's lap, Wolfgang and Judith in their own secret world, Beth and Guy poring over a map and all of us silent as Sean, gripping the wheel tightly, his knuckles white, throws the bus into gear and roars down the road. I notice that sweat is now pouring down his face. He is going far too fast and is driving almost recklessly, but looking at his expression, I don't like to say anything, so I hang on to my seat with both hands as he makes a wide sweep around the bend.

The bang, when it comes, throws me forward onto the rail in front of me, which saves me from tumbling out of the open door. A loud shriek from Edna and she has fallen forward onto her knees into the aisle between the back seats. Bags skid along the floor and pile up against the front before I watch one fly past and out of the doorway. Then, that moment of stunned silence before everyone begins moving and talking at once. Fortunately we are all unhurt, apart from Edna, whose knees are red and beginning to bruise, though the skin is unbroken. Her great weight needs four of us to get her back on her feet again and we sit her back in her seat with Phoebe and Beth either side, one fanning her while the other opens a bottle of water.   The landslide is big with boulders strewn right across the road but the front of the bus doesn't look that badly damaged, although the engine had cut out immediately on impact. Now I watch, horrified, as Sean, standing in the middle of the road, crumbles before me. Covering his eyes with both hands, he begins to sob like a small child. And I thought this guy was dependable in a crisis!

"I'm so sorry, Chloe. It's all my fault!" he snivels and wipes his nose on his bare arm. Standing in front of the bus, he tries to pull himself together as men begin to appear from out of nowhere. A few minutes ago it was a deserted road but now bare feet come running from across the fields, pounding around the corner and down a nearby track to the left. In minutes we are surrounded. The crowd all talk together in Hindi so I can't understand a word. Two of them climb onto the bus. Sean just stands there looking lost and pathetic. Well, someone needs to take charge.

Miss Jean Brodie?

"Look. It's not that bad! We just need to get the bus towed away to a garage and then we need to be taken back to where we've just come from. It's not such a big deal." Do I sound convincing? I don't really have a clue what I am talking about but no one else knows what to do either!

Wolfgang and then William and Guy join me. A new man has just joined the throng around us. "Please, madam, to come with me. There is a *parao*, a rest house here just nearby."

So we collect our bags and follow him along the hot and dusty track, the girls helping a valiant but lame Edna. And so it is that, instead of making our way along the road to Varanasi, we spend the next four hours in an old government rest house where time has just stood captive over the years. Unused but watched over by a boy who serves us mint tea and shows us around. There is a bed to rest on and Edna takes it, but who knows how long since it was last slept upon? When the sheets were last changed? The rest of us sit and rest out of the midday heat until eventually a jeep comes to pick us up and take us back into Kajuraho. The bus is still stranded forlornly in the middle of the road but we are taken back in the direction from where we came. Back to Kajuraho, and no sign of Sean.

Two days pass while we wait for news on the bus. Bhaskar is back, or perhaps he never left? Sean stays isolated in his room with Bhaskar running around for him, carrying messages and sorting out arrangements to get the bus taken further on to the nearest mechanic.

I use this time to explore the village and befriend Anu. She is an orphan, only ten years old but she lives alone with her six younger brothers and sisters in a small mud hut with a twig roof and a small porch on which stands the one string bed. Inside, the hut is empty except for a shelf with a few pots, a string stretching across from one wall to the other holding a few rags of clothes and a floor covered in fresh goat droppings. She shoos the goat out of the way and shyly gestures to me to sit on the bed. She shows me her exercise book and pencil from school and somehow we manage to talk together, mostly because she speaks a little English, although I do now have a Hindu phrase book to help. While we sit side by side on the bed, one of her sisters gathers up the goat dung in her hands off the floor; later she will mix it with straw, shape it into large cakes and leave it to dry. Then it becomes fuel for the cooking fire. Anu scolds, soothes and hugs all the little ones in turn and they all shriek with laughter when the naked baby pees all over me. All of them have head lice and flies sit around their eyes. Although there is no adult living with them the extended village family live in the other six huts not far from the roadside.

When I leave them to walk back to the shop, they all accompany me as far as the hostel gate, walking in the road and doubling up with laughter when I take the verge. From their hilarious gestures I know I have just walked along the women's toilet route and, looking down, I can tell they are right and remove myself quickly, glad that I am not barefoot! We pass a new bridegroom with his head of hennaed hair. Sensual women, caste marks on their foreheads, stained lips and hennaed hands, wearing toe rings on their slim bare feet, walk alongside me chattering, their nose studs catching the sunlight.

At the same small store on the edge of the village I buy two bars of soap for Anu and her family and lots of apples, oranges and bananas from the street vendor outside. On my way back a young man riding alongside me on a bicycle suggests a visit to the local Holy Man – "where we can smoke marijuana" – and offers me betel to chew. As I know that the betel nut is sometimes mixed with opium, I decide not to take his offer though now I wish I had tried it just the once. It is the red-stained teeth of the regular betel user that puts me off.

Around four o'clock we are all sitting on the sparse grass of the hostel garden waiting for a bleary-eyed Sean to give us an update on the condition of the bus, which he tells us should be repaired by tomorrow or the day after. He doesn't trust the mechanic and hopes we can make it as far as Varanasi.

I am writing this travel journal as the sun goes down, Rosie's photo propped up beside me along with the papier-mache elephant and the butterfly necklace. A tap on the door and Sean steps into my room and sits down on the only chair. "Chloe, I need to tell you something." I wait for him to go on and he just comes right out with it. "I'm a heroin addict. I can't drive any more. I'm suffering cold turkey. That's why

I crashed the bus. I didn't want to do this trip. It always takes me weeks to recover and I've had enough of it."

Silenced, I sit and wait for him to continue.

"Will you help me?"

What? Me? Help him? It takes a second to take in what he's saying. He sits there, hands hanging loosely down at his side, head dropped. He doesn't look up at me. Instead of the stocky, strong guy I first met, I see a weak and helpless soul. In a second, a fiercely ardent Chloe, on her knees and impulsively throwing her arms around him, holds him tight. ("Think before you act." My father's weekly drilling is completely forgotten, those lines he made me write a hundred times now making little impression, though my fingers sometimes ached afterwards.)

"I wanted to tell you. Haven't you noticed the soldiers with the guns?" His voice is muffled against my shoulder. Now I remember I wanted to ask someone about that. "Well, there's no heroin available here in Kajuraho because of their presence. When the bus crashed I was desperate and then we had to come back." And he looks as if he might cry again at any moment. Help him? I don't know how to find heroin!

"Listen, Sean. I'm sorry but I wouldn't know what heroin even looks like and even if I did, I couldn't get you any."

"No, Chloe, you don't understand." And he makes a face. "I want to stop. I want you to help me stop."

Together we share a cigarette in the silence of the evening. Then Sean simply gets up and goes from my room without another word spoken between us, leaving me to a restless night.

Just before dawn I get up and watch the sunrise and she

brings with her the solution. As the shuffling sideways movement, the nose that almost touches the ground, the strong man's hands and tiny feet come into mind, I suddenly know the answer. I will help and travel on with Sean. Edna's warning is forgotten.

Chapter 7

"I knew he was your man all the time, honey." Edna digs me in the ribs with her dimpled elbow as she goes down the path to the gate. "I have to warn you, though, it won't be an easy path. I had a quick look in my crystal ball last night and I see trouble ahead. I'm sorry, honey."

In voluminous purple with a turban to match, she is flirting outrageously with the shy young man who carries her bag to the waiting taxi. Saying goodbye to Judith and Wolfgang and being taken again into those ample lavender hills that are Edna's bosom, I watch as all three climb into the rickshaw that will take them to the bus station. Edna, limping a bit with her bad knee, needs help as she knocks her hat and it tips forward over her eyes as she gets in. Judith goes around to assist her from the other side and Edna suddenly plops back into the seat like a blancmange popping out of its mould. There is a noise like a whoopee cushion fart as she goes down and the driver looks a little alarmed at the sight of his rickshaw sinking heavily on one side with this extra weight. Then she leans forward immediately to wave frantically, "Bye Miss Chloe, honey", and keeps it up until they have gone around the corner and disappeared out of sight. Her fluttering hand, with today's purple nails, is a lasting image. The moment's quiet brings with it the reflection that I shall miss her. Her eccentricity adds a rare flavour to any group gathering. Besides, how could you ever forget someone who meets Clark Gable in the bathroom each night?

The other four come wandering through the gate and, after saying our goodbyes, they saunter off down the road, hoping to hitch another lift. Travelling around India brings them no concerns. The soldier, standing nearby, shifts his gun to the other shoulder and shows little interest in any of us as he chats to the small and inevitable crowd of men and boys now gathered in front of the hostel. When they have all left I go up to collect Sean, who is lying on top of his bed with no sign of Bhaskar. Perhaps he has already left? The windows are closed and the air is stale with the smell of bed and sweat as I pull back the curtains and open the windows wide. The sun floods the room as he makes a huge effort to drag himself up.

We walk slowly side by side down the road to the local telegraph office or telephone exchange, situated in a small corrugated tin hut in the middle of the village. A uniformed man in khaki sits behind a table in this humid fly infested space with its chairs with their broken seats, leaving us to perch on their outside edges, while we wait our turn. The room is full of curious people sitting around on the floor, most of them covered in the flies, which hang in a thick cloud in the middle like gnats over a pond. Fortunately the uniformed guy speaks some English so I give him the number of U Go Overland and we sit and wait. A lot of winding, twiddling knobs, and shouting goes on until eventually we are told there are no lines today. Disappointed because we had psyched ourselves up to talk to James back in the office, it's a meek Sean who walks back alongside me

"Chloe, haven't you noticed that wherever we've been, I'm greeted by men who seem to know me well?"

My mind goes back to that first evening in New Delhi and the filthy restaurant and the men waving goodbye from the door, then the sightings of Sean in the mosque and on the back of the motorbike in Jaipur. It is all beginning to make some kind of sense. And the moods. Yes. Particularly the changing moods. But then I remember something else. The money! What about all the money? The brown package I brought with me and which he was so eager to get his hands on, and the fares paid by the others when they came on board. But in an instant I really know what's happened to the money and don't need him to explain. "There's no money to repair the bus, Chloe." He looks ashamed. Sweat runs down his face and and neck he looks as if he might be sick. I leave him at the door to his room and I go back to the village.

On my way to Anu's hut, two men pass me as they go to the river carrying a dead child: a girl of about ten years dressed in a faded blue robe that hangs towards the ground from her limp body. Her head is tilted back but her eyes are closed and her expression peaceful.

"*Namaste!*" a woman standing at the roadside calls and gestures to me to come across and invites me into her home. One of several small houses off the narrow street. A room that just contains the three string beds placed around the walls. Two shelves hold the cooking pots and along one side is a short wooden staircase, more like a ladder, that disappears into some kind of loft or more sleeping spaces. There are photographs of her daughters, which she shows me, pulling them out of the shiny aluminium tin trunk from under one of the beds. Head and shoulders photos of two dark-haired beauties, like their mother, the bright red of the caste mark contrasting with the deep colours of their saris. Pushpa herself is wearing pale coffee-coloured cotton with bands of drawn thread work around the short-sleeved top and the edges and hem of the sari. She is a handsome and sensual woman with her jewelled arms and bare feet with their painted nails and rings and the scent of patchouli that follows her around as she makes the tea. She takes fresh mint from the bunch out of the basket hanging from a nail in the ceiling then she collects water in a jug from the communal tap outside and almost opposite.

We sit on the beds and sip the boiling and fragrant tea from small glasses. However, it soon becomes clear that one of Pushpa's daughters is in urgent need of a typewriter so, after promising to make some enquiries, I duck my head under the low door, leave her home and continue on down the dirt street. As I get near to the huts the children run up to greet me and take the apples from my bag. The smallest boy must be about fourteen months and is naked except for a thin leather string around his waist with a good luck charm, like a coin, situated somewhere around his tummy button. They pass him to me as they munch on apples, breaking off pieces to put in his mouth.

Anu, just back from her morning school, shows me her new English words. A happy hour flies by as we play together and giggle and they encourage me to make a 'poo' cake from the dung, showing me how to mix it with the dried grass. A very smelly time, with runny green goats' dung almost up to my elbows, but I am proud of my handiwork when I see it put to dry beside the others. A little misshapen, perhaps, but not bad for a beginner! (Back in New York, which seems light years away, I would only have to flick a switch to bring instant heating.) Anu brings me some water and the bar of soap I had brought her, as well as a rag to wash and dry my hands.

Together we walk back, me carrying a contented baby gurgling on my hip. The little orphans carrying their own unique joy. At the hostel they leave me at the gates and I watch them skip away with awe in my heart.

The next morning Sean and I repeat our walk down to the tin hut and, after ten minutes of trying, we get through. The uniformed man hands him the old-fashioned bakelite phone while all the others get up off the floor and gather around us to listen as even more men saunter through the door and join us. At the other end James is beside himself with fury. Sean remains remarkably calm, his voice strong, though his body shakes as he confesses, "The truth is, I'm a junkie, James. I can't continue with this trip."

I can hear James shouting. We all can. "Are you crazy? She'll sue us!" Sean hands the phone to me. The sweat is pouring down his face. "This is very inconvenient. I leave for Iran tomorrow. There's nothing I can do," James rushes on without stopping or allowing me to speak. "Most inconsiderate. I'm a very busy man!" I picture him smoking and pacing up and down the office in East Grinstead and now, as he bangs the receiver down, I remember the last time with the phone falling on the floor. (Hey! I'm the client, remember?) Really, this is crazy! First a ramshackle bus, then no other passengers and now a driver who is in no condition to drive anywhere and, on top of this, the bus is broken and we have no money to mend it. The small print on U Go Overland's brochure says they will replace a driver should one go sick. Well, Sean's right: the company must be in the shit!

Now Sean says, "They're not affiliated so you have no protection, Chloe, no way of forcing them to replace me. I'm sorry." Affiliated? Innocent me knows nothing about travel companies being affiliated. "Tomorrow we'll ring again and speak to Claude, who runs the office in James's absence. I'll ask him to telegraph money out. We can collect it in Varanasi," he continues convincingly,

"But you aren't in any condition to drive, Sean!"

"No. I wasn't planning to!"

As the penny drops I have to laugh out loud. "You can't be *serious*? I can't drive a bus! I wouldn't know how! The most I've ever driven is a small car!" The very thought of it brings knots into my stomach and fills me with anxiety.

"Driving around New York must be a nightmare. I'm sure if you can do that, you can drive along these roads. Chloe, the bus will be impounded if we leave it here. The least I can do for James is to get it to Kathmandu and with your help, I can. Then once it's safely parked up there I can fly back to England. I can't do this alone, Chloe. Please help." And those green Irish eyes aren't dancing as they look into mine

"But a *bus*, Sean!"

"Courage, Chloe!" And he touches my shoulder with his shaking fingers.

That word 'courage' always makes me think of my other high school friend, Julie, whose life so slowly slipped away two years ago. Her courage and laughter as we clung to each other in her hospital bed have never stopped amazing me. I knew if she were here now she wouldn't hesitate for a second. "Go for it, kiddo." I can almost hear her say it.

So I do go for it. And that's how I find myself digging into my pocket for my bankcard to pay for the repairs to the bus – "just until we reach Varanasi."

"Take it steadily," Sean warns, quite unnecessarily. I have eased the clutch out and am lurching slowly away from the hostel just as waving children run down the road towards us. At least the bush telegraph works well! Slamming my foot down hard on the brake pedal, both of us are thrown forward. "Jesus, Chloe, d'you want to get us both killed?" I see the irony is lost on him so say nothing but wave back and start again, the little ones running behind the bus as we limp out of Kajuraho. The effort and concentration I need to drive this unaccustomed length and size of vehicle make it impossible to talk, so Sean sits tensely opposite the open door, looking white and ghastly, while I pray that we will meet little traffic and no more landslides as I grip the wheel tightly and manoeuvre the bends.

A silent half hour passes.

"There's a Holy Man at the top of the next hill, we can stop if you'd like to." He is all affable suddenly, wanting to please. Well, a short break would be good and besides, I haven't met any of these Holy Men yet.

At the top he tells me to pull over to the side and then moves across me to keep his foot on the brake pedal. Going to stand in the doorway of the bus, I watch as an old and tattered man in faded white, his beard long and thin, like his hair, comes towards me from behind a large rock. In his hand he carries a dish of small chopped up pieces, the size of dice, of something hard and dry looking. A few flies are hovering around the dish, no doubt peeing all over those unappetising morsels, as he gestures to me to take several pieces and put them in my mouth. They taste old and stale and a bit like desiccated coconut, but no matter, as they will bring me good luck (or deli belly perhaps?) His pale watery eyes hold mine and he raises one hand in blessing over my head. Into the other I put the necessary rupees. "You will have safe journey now and very, very happy days are coming to you." I remember the offer to smoke marijuana with the Holy Man in Kajuraho, and can't help wondering what this Holy Man will be spending his rupees on! He stands there, a frail figure, watching as I nervously pull out and back into the road.

We bump along for a bit until I get back into the rhythm, but after only a few short miles and a climb up to the top of another hill, there is a loud and hissing explosion as the radiator loses all its water. So much for the Holy Man's predictions!

It takes us hours and many detours before we find a dodgy mechanic to help. In the meantime, we stop and fill the radiator every mile or so from the water can Sean carries in the back of the bus. It's so hot and the seat beneath me is wringing wet when we stop, once, for mint tea, served at the side of the road and once, so that I can quickly crouch behind a bush – keeping a sharp look-out for cobras. The mechanic does a very temporary job so when we get onto the highway we are still stopping to fill the radiator, though not quite as often as before. My head aches from the relentless heat and the stress of having to concentrate so hard.

Meanwhile, Sean is a pleasant companion again and there is a relaxed easiness between us that wasn't there before. He is almost pathetically grateful and wanting to please me. "Chloe, you just tell me now if there's anything you particularly want to see." What an opportunity I now have with this experienced guide willing to take me anywhere I want to go! (Julie, if you could see me now you'd be proud of me!) I break into song, oblivious to Sean's obvious discomfort and, apart from the radiator stops, we cruise along effortlessly.

It's an exhausted but satisfied and very smug Chloe who pulls up outside the grubby and small hotel in Rewa.

"You need to stop driving, Chloe. I think you've done enough for today." Sean is right. My head is thumping well now and besides, he doesn't look too good either. Two men immediately approach us from across the street and greet Sean, inclining their heads towards me and joining their hands. "*Namaste.*" Immediately Sean pinches my arm and I know that these men are waiting to sell him heroin. They both reek of alcohol and the shorter of the two is unsteady on his feet. The taller one invites Sean for a beer and gestures to a shack across the road.

"Chloe." His voice is barely audible as, turning his head away from them, he whispers near my ear, "I'm sorry, but I really need you to help me right now and besides, I don't want to drink a beer!" Not that I had been included in the invitation.

120

"Anyway I thought you were trying to give up drugs?" I say, turning my gaze from Sean towards the two men. "Sean won't be drinking with you or buying from you. He's trying to kick the habit so perhaps it's better if you go away. Now, can we please find our rooms? Are you coming, Sean?" And without looking at his face, I sweep past him and climb the steps to the entrance hall, wondering if I did OK. When I hear footsteps following, I know that this time all is well.

The grim, moustached young man sitting just inside on the floor gets up reluctantly and leads us along a dark and dirty corridor to a door at the end on the left hand side. It is a large room with badly broken double windows leading onto a veranda that runs around the outside. Four more men are sitting cross-legged on the wooden deck and looking none too friendly as they see me peering out. An indescribable shower room with raw sewage seeping up through the grid of the drain hole makes me gag and when I pull the sheet back on the nearest bed, it is soiled and stinking.

"Please change this bed, I am not sleeping in this filth!" With newfound confidence Miss Jean Brodie almost shouts into that insolent face. He simply takes the top sheet off and rolls it into a bundle without a word.

"Sean, I don't like this place. It doesn't feel very safe. There's no lock and those men outside can just walk in here off the veranda."

"I know. This is one of the places the company uses and has an agreement with. Only costs thirty-five English pence a night. That's why they use it. I'm sorry. Look, there are three beds in here, Chloe. How about I take one of them?"

Looking at his worn out face, I don't know who might

protect whom but it will certainly make me feel better to have him nearby. After discovering that there are taps but no water, we give up on any ideas of cleanliness and go down into the street and buy samosas. It's just a small wooden stall but from it emanates the most captivating smells so that by the time I hold the crisp cumin-scented parcel in my hand, I am ravenous again. We remain outside, watching as the sun goes down, curious groups of men watching us. As always, my thoughts ramble towards Rosie, Mike and my mother too is now included. With that glimpse of the young woman she once was, she gave herself away. Just as she once gave her life away and lost sight of it. Well, I shall share this journal with her at the end of my trip and maybe we can recapture some of that cosiness of the other week.

A large shadow leaves by the long windows and slips into the dark night as we enter the bedroom. The bed has not been remade but the room smells cleaner. Someone has obviously used some lavender air spray. Reminds me of Edna. But I still feel uneasy. There is something here that is not quite right and for the first time, the people seem unfriendly. Neither of us undresses but lie on top of the beds fully clothed, alert and listening to the low murmurings coming from the veranda.

Sean gets up at about midnight to pace up and down while I try to get some sleep, but it's impossible so I sit up and we chat, Sean on the end of my bed.

"I can't continue to live my life like this, Chloe, and I'll never do this trip again. When I get back to England I always have to shut myself up for about six weeks to come down off it. I told James I didn't want to do the Indian trip again."

"But Sean why *did* you do it? You can't ever save any money!"

"I wanted to take the Iranian trip but James insists on doing that one himself." His face is miserable but then the lines blur and change and I am aware of a prickling sensation up my spine and I am looking into the face, not of Sean but of the Crab Man. As the blurring starts again, the lines ripple like the reflection in a pool and the contours settle back once more into the now familiar shape that is Sean.

"Why are you looking at me like that, Chloe?"

His question startles me. "Like what?" I am confused by these strange new sensations.

"Like you're looking at an object of love, I suppose." He is embarrassed and goes bright red.

"Well, you *are* an object of love, aren't you?" The words rush out of my mouth. "There's always something beautiful to find inside somewhere, isn't there? Its just a question of looking." Is this *me* talking? This schmaltzy talk?

"You look like a small child on her birthday, Chloe! Where's all this coming from all of a sudden?" And he smiles. "Come on. We need to try and sleep." I don't answer him as we very naturally curl up together, our arms around each other. Because I know where it came from. We stay like that till morning, when we hurriedly get up and leave this strange place behind.

Driving along the highway to Varanasi, a terrible thing happens. I can't avoid what I think is a pile of rags in the road, only to realise that it is in fact the remains of a boy's body. I think I am going to be sick. "I can't do this any more, Sean. I'm sorry. We'll just have to find another way," I groan as, deeply shocked and disgusted with myself, I sit on the roadside and refuse to get back into the driver's seat, not wanting to look at the bit of a small arm protruding from the ragged and bloodstained cloths. "I mean, how can they do that? Just leave a body in the road? How can life be so cheap? We need to do something. But what?"

"Life is an eternal circle here, Chloe – like many of the traditions, Hinduism believes in the eternal cycle of life and death. Through death comes rebirth into another new life and so life just goes on in one form or another. He was probably an orphan so there would have been no one to put his body in the river."

"But shouldn't we do something now? We can't just leave him to be run over again and again." While we've been speaking, two vultures have landed and begin pecking at the bundle until a lorry's hooting sends them flapping back to the other side of the road.

"There's nothing for us to do here. Get back into the bus." His voice is firm. Not like his hands, which tremble violently. I am not convinced but miserably I have to agree. Now it's Sean who takes the wheel for the last few miles while I wonder about that discarded child.

As we approach this ancient and most holy of cities, we pass many men carrying dead bodies on bamboo stretchers, as they make their slow way to the most sacred of all rivers, the Ganga or Ganges.

There is no money waiting for us at the bank in Varanasi and another call to Claude at U Go Overland is put through from the main post office, a big, clean and bright building. It is clear that no money has yet been sent but Sean promises that there *will* be money waiting in Kathmandu. I don't know what to do. U Go Overland has already conned me once. "Trust me, Chloe, I'll make sure you get your money." Now he looks at me and I want to believe him. Am I being naïve? Too trusting? But for now, his gaze is clear as his eyes hold mine.

Leaving the bus with the mechanic, we make our way on foot to a small guesthouse, where the air conditioning brings sweet relief from the sun's burning rays as we take adjoining rooms with a connecting door. I know that Sean now finds sleep eludes him so this arrangement will give us an opportunity for middle-of-the-night chats.

More and more exotic sights to see and emotions to feel make me wonder how much overwhelming a person's senses can take. The boundaries of my mind are being pushed ever further. Perhaps it is limitless.

Varanasi, or Benares as the Indians call her, is one of the oldest and most holy living cities in the world. Also known as Kashi, or the 'City of Light', it pulses and throbs whichever way you turn. I can hardly wait to go to the Ghats but Sean proposes a boat trip at dawn to observe the morning rituals. So, for now, I just have to savour the anticipation and be patient. We visit a silk shop where once again Sean is greeted like an old friend. Although I watch closely, I don't see or overhear any deals being made and Sean appears relaxed. I find myself, the only woman, seated on a cushion inside a small, open-sided room. A small clay bowl of some kind of alcohol on the floor beside me. Four men, also seated, listen to the sweet sounds coming from the sitar played by the young man cross-legged on the other side. Surrounding us, walls made up of bales of silk of every shade. Against this kaleidoscopic backcloth we stay till late and as the last sounds die away there is a moment of digestion and silent appreciation. Picking our way back along the night streets, where sleeping bodies lie on string beds pulled out onto the roadside, I cannot imagine ever being able to sleep with all this wonder in my soul, but I drift off on my carpet of magic thoughts and images of the Crab Man.

Am I part of an epic film set? Our little boat bobs up and down on this sacred river flowing directly from the foot of God; the flowers and candles I have bought from the sari clad women on the riverside floating alongside us. The pink rays of the dawn sun just showing in the sky and the five kilometres of stone steps, known as the Ghats, shimmering mystically before us. A giant palette of colour as pilgrims make their way to the river's edge to bathe. Behind them the tops of temples, domes and minarets of mosques. Closer to the steps, the old buildings carrying the tidemark from last year's swelling water. In the distance, to the right, the 'burning Ghat' where small fires of various woods burn and cremate the bodies, the air filled with the smell of resin mingled with incense and oil lamps. Brahmins in white congregate in one area; in another, women in all their beautiful saris enter the water and wash themselves. In yet another, young men sit and do yoga. Bloated bodies float, vultures atop, and a dead baby tied to a stone is rowed past, but nothing can detract from this huge and brilliant scene of seething humanity in all her shapes and sizes. Sean tells me that to burn a body takes five hours, the ashes being taken by the men into the river after an elaborate ritual. Now we watch as these take place. I have no idea how long we spend out on the water. I only know that when I step ashore again

I have just experienced something completely compelling and unforgettable, indelibly stamped somewhere within my being.

As the baser feeling of hunger hits us, we make our way through the priests and flower sellers, past the brassware and silk shops, to find a place to sit and eat a curry breakfast. There are seemingly no secrets between us now and it's easy to talk with Sean. We walk through the women sorting the sacred Tulsi plants preparing for the folk celebration and celestial marriage ceremony on the next full moon. Sean tells me about the two types of Tulsi – Rama Tulsi and Krishna Tulsi – and the mythical story behind this ancient tradition performed by the women on the banks of this holiest of rivers. Soon, on "the eleventh day from no moon day", the two plants will be united. The Tulsi plant, a type of basil found in every Indian home, is revered both for its medicinal and spiritual properties. When the branches are added to the funeral pyre they keep the insects at bay and ensure the journey of the soul back to Source. Within the flowering sprigs is said to reside the Goddess Lakshmi, consort of Vishnu, the Creator. After a terrible curse was put upon her, Vishnu intervened. "You will live in the world as a Tulsi plant and when the curse has run its course you will come back to me." By caring for this sacred plant, the women are creating a bond with the Tulasi, the archetype of femininity, representing the virtue and sorrow of all women. "O Goddess Tulsi. I beseech you to protect the lives of my family and the spirits of those who have died." Soon, these women will celebrate the phenomenon of merging human existence with celestial figures and becoming one with God. How I wish I could still be here to witness this sacred marriage.

That merging of the worlds. My vegetable thali grows cold through listening.

That afternoon we call back to the mechanic. Glad of the chance to catch my thoughts I sit in the shade until attacked by angry monkeys from behind. "Quick, Chloe!" Sean pulls me up just in time as a particularly vicious monkey leaps at my head from the tree. Apart from a long scratch down one arm, I am unharmed but glad to get onto the fully repaired bus and away from angry animals. The bus still carries Edna's perfume and today, for some reason, it seems particularly strong. Finding my credit card again to pay for the repairs, I drop my wallet under the seat and have to get down on my knees to retrieve it. There, rolling around on the floor, is a tiny phial of Lavender oil. Edna's!

Two more days of exploring this breathless city, its temples, its mosques, its sacred shrines, and we are finally ready to move on again. Every so often Sean is recognised and approached by various men but he never leaves my side. Bossy Jean Brodie tells them to "run along" as he won't be doing business. Our last night we take a gentle walk at dusk along the narrow streets, savouring smells and sounds and storing pictures in that secret place inside of me. Suddenly startled, I catch the swish of ample violet hips entering the small dark shop we are passing. Surely it *can't* be? Peering to get a closer look, I see a purple turban disappearing through a door to the back, hear the loud southern drawl, the laugh like a hyena. *Edna!* What is the old girl up to now? Another massage? Intrigued, but we don't disturb her rendezvous and walk on under the stars.

For a while, at least until we are out of the city, Sean agrees to drive. We are on our way to Senauli where we will cross the border into Nepal and take the long English/Chinese road into that country. We settle back into silence, me in my usual position near the open door. Can it really only be a few weeks ago that I left New York and then England? Who is this woman sitting beside this man? Whoever she is – she feels alert, excited, unafraid and very much alive.

Chapter 8

If, of thy worldly goods thou art bereft
And, of thy slender store, two loaves alone are left,
Sell one – and with the dole
Buy hyacinths to feed thy soul.

(Omar Khayyam)

Well, my soul is so overfed it doesn't need hyacinths. A new taste of freedom in my mouth from a lifetime diet of petty constraints, rules, regulations and power trips, designed to crush and control the spirit from its inward journeying, its outward expression. My thoughts roam, my heart sings and I am anonymous. With no-one's expectations to live up to it's easy to relax and just 'be', although the walk towards the distant jungle across the lush green paddy fields is long and hard because of the heat.

The men are all working in the fields so Sean is the only adult male presence when we go to meet Bhaskar's family. Of Bhaskar himself I have seen nothing since we left Kajaraho. These women have never seen a white woman's face before and they surround me, touching my clothes and face with delight. I tower above them like the giant I feel but they draw me into the bosom of their huge family and ply me with offers of food and drink. The cool water with its slice of lime poured from the spotless stainless steel jug helps stem my thirst. Enormous fans made from rushes are brought out and my perspiring face is fanned with their soft breeze. We converse with nods and even miming when it's difficult to get a point across. Love moves between us, weaving her strands back and forth. The photographs taken against the jungle backcloth show me towering above this cheerful family group, my Punjabi suit looking grubby and soaked with sweat marks, but we all wear broad grins. It is with regret that I leave them and make the return walk back to the bus with a worn out Sean, the effort of walking in the heat making him grumpy.

At the border village of Senauli I share a wooden room with the biggest cockroaches ever, while next door is a whole family who cook outside on the wooden deck underneath my window. I watch the *lassi* drink of fermenting curd being stirred in a bucket by two squatting men who use their bare hands and arms to swish the white liquid around. I have been drinking the delicious *lassi*, with all its beneficial bacteria, on a daily basis but now I am not quite sure.

This place somehow reminds me of the old mining town in Madrid in New Mexico, with its dirt road and cluster of food stalls with their steaming cooking pots, wooden trestle tables to eat at and cut-price booze shacks to drink in. A first gin and tonic slips down easily, then another.

As dusk gathers, a walk across the twenty feet or so of 'no man's land' and back into India to visit a family where elderly members are already settling for the night outside the thatched hut and a child lies, breathing gently, underneath a mosquito net. Inside we jostle for space on the earth floor and sit on our haunches, crowded together, listening to modern but unknown pop music on the cassette player Sean carried across with him. The thin small man with the dark moustache and sunken cheeks is an old friend of his, it seems. I don't catch his name. The volume is turned up high and there is little conversation. The music pounds out into the night sky while the small children sleep and the old people try to look interested. Mosquitoes are biting and the floor is hard but I wouldn't miss a moment. Later, crossing back into Senauli, Sean is stopped and the cassette player taken from him. There is just one sleepy guy on watch by the small hut. He flips the cassette deck open and shut again before handing the player back. When Sean takes it I notice how his hand shakes. He must be exhausted. It's been another long day.

It's one o'clock before I climb on top of my bed, leaving the floor space to the cockroaches. The sounds of the night carry through the small window and thin walls. Sean taps on the connecting wall and I respond. In four hours I will get up and take a taxi to the Buddha's pool in Lumbini. Sometime in the night the Crab Man smiles at me and speaks, but I remember nothing of what he says.

The Olympic-type flame burns constantly close to the pool the baby Buddha and his mother bathed in. I am always so very early for any appointment and this morning is no exception. I find I am completely alone and spend time quietly in the small shrine where my forehead is anointed with dye. I only meet this one monk although there is a monastery full of them here. Being solitary after the last few weeks is welcome and standing beside the water in this one truly authenticated religious site, I feel deeply touched. The water shimmers with my reflection and a sudden shadow behind me. Turning swiftly to catch whomever it is, all I see is parched grass and a few trees. No one about. Walking back to the taxi, my mind is full of the Crab Man again and a fierce desire to see him. Understand more. Who he really is seems to be connected with who I really am, although that doesn't make much sense even to me, who has the thought. And that's another thing – *is* there such a thing as original thought?

The long drive to Kathmandu passes without much conversation. Sean seems to have withdrawn again and although he now takes his turn to drive, he is tense and stressed and often swears voraciously and for no apparent reason. The spectacular scenery can only be enjoyed as a passenger, since the road is steep and the ravines lying below us deep and alarmingly full of wrecked buses. Sometimes log cabins perch drunkenly on the edge high above the frothing white water, the shouts of the brave rafters rising up to reach us. The people's faces begin to look more Tibetan with their almond-shaped eyes. Kathmandu, when we reach it, is bustling and cosmopolitan but seems at odds with the Nepalese culture and traditions. German cake shops, Mohican hairstyles and tie-dyed clothes don't seem to my mind to mix easily with orange-robed monks and the daily mountain life of the poverty stricken Nepalese.

At last the bus is safely manoeuvred into a compound where we leave it with a sense of a mission finally accomplished.

It also feels a little flat as shortly I shall be on my own and this part of my journey has come to an end. And what a journey it has been! We relax in a coffee shop with a plate of scrummy looking cakes between us. Neither of us saying much. I look across at Sean and catch him staring at me. He looks quickly away and clears his throat, about to say something; instead, after a short awkward silence, he gets up to pay.

A visit to the bank brings the now almost expected answer. No money. He can't meet my eyes as he asks me to help him pay his fare back to England and promises to send the money back immediately on his return there. "Claude says he hasn't had the time to make the transfer but I'll go straight to the office myself and make sure he does it." His eyes on the ground. What is all this? I don't understand what is happening here. Do the company have any money at all if they are going bankrupt? Rosie would be so cross with me. She would probably tell Sean to get lost. Seeing me hesitate, he suggests I ring Claude myself and confirm this new arrangement they seem to have agreed between them. It takes ten minutes to get through but Claude is affable enough, apologetic even, been snowed under with bookings (can I believe *that*?) and agrees that I will be fully compensated for all the expenses. Well, Sean has got me this far on my journey but, by the look of him, it's time he left. Ignoring Edna's warning for a second time, a ticket is bought, a flight booked. Meanwhile, I agree to wait in Kathmandu until the money reaches the bank.

Next morning I watch Sean get on the bus, which will take him to the airport. He turns his head away and climbs aboard.

A hunched and miserable figure. At the last moment he puts out an arm to touch my shoulder and looks straight at me. "Thanks, Chloe. I promise to send you the money tomorrow." Then he bends forward and for a just a second his lips brush mine. So swift I almost imagined it. I wave hard until the bus is out of sight but he never turns around. His going has already left a noticeable gap. We have shared a lot these few weeks and become close in a way. Like fellow conspirators.

Next, it's my turn to take a bus trip back but not before I have passed a shop with photographs of Everest and made the quick decision to go up into the mountains and to Nagarkot.

A frightening pot-holed road, the bus swinging violently from side to side to avoid the worst ones, makes it a nerve-racking ride. The edge and the abyss of the ravine never far out of sight. The last part made more safely on foot. Another wooden hut lit by the moon and with just a bucket to fetch water to wash in. One of a small cluster of huts sitting down among the wild flowered beauty, snow-covered Everest in front of me.

Magic arrives with the sun next morning as she cloaks that majesty with her rays and later on floods the whole valley. My day is spent walking, exploring, and thinking. A rough wooden sign points towards the Restaurant at the End of the World where the one table doubles up as both bed for the owner to sleep on and table for guests to eat off. A simple but welcome meal. Lying contentedly on the grass nearby looking up towards the bright blue of the sky, I have time to let my thoughts go and I watch them as they fly across a wide variety of themes.

Mahabala plops down beside me. Thirty-six years old and

a teacher, he supports his whole family. He fell in love years ago with a German girl but never dared to touch her or tell her. He tells me he longs to break the chains. He refused an arranged marriage, couldn't contemplate buying a wife and has no sexual experience. Yet another soul bound by conventional thinking. I can only encourage him to break the chains, think for himself and start to fly. (Did I really say all that to a complete stranger?) I leave him finishing a bottle of rum and leaving it "all to God". But perhaps, just sometimes, God likes to see us doing something for ourselves.

My hair is filthy and, besides, I have never washed it in a bucket before and really want the experience. Whilst collecting my shampoo, I see a familiar looking man coming out from the hut next to mine. Where have I seen that face before? Before I can ask him, he walks off quickly in the opposite direction but I catch him later over a cup of mint tea in the café that belongs to this small rustic complex of dwellings.

"Don't I know you from somewhere? My name's Chloe." And I extend my hand. He looks surprised but non-committal and then it dawns on me! Of course! The photo Claude had shown me of the guy from Australia, what was his name – Jim? "You're Jim, aren't you?"

"Yes, you're quite right." He clasps my hand. "Missed the bus trip, I'm afraid, so made it on up here." Just like the photograph. Middle-aged, a little overweight but a pleasant face, nice eyes. Doesn't have much of an accent though. Sounds more English. My story about no passengers and driving the bus trip tumbles out over tea though I just tell him that Sean collapsed and was unwell. He seems concerned, which I think I find rather sweet of him.

"Well, what are your plans now, Chloe?" he asks when I finally pause for breath.

"Back to Kathmandu to wait for the money transfer and then on to Calcutta and then…" I am not ready to voice my return to Delhi and the Crab Man. Besides, I am not sure anyone could understand and certainly not a regular guy like Jim. "Er, maybe Bombay. You know, that's the place they make all the movies, isn't it?"

We talk until its time for a simple dinner – correction, I talk until I can't think of another thing to say and finally get around to ask him about himself. Having taken early retirement, he is on his way to England to visit his elderly mother in her flat in Hove. An accountant from Perth, married twenty years but divorced for four. Childhood sweethearts until one of them grew up and the other one didn't. He soon switches the conversation back to me, sits back and looks interested in all I have to say. A good listener. Eventually, the boy asks us to leave, as he wants to close the café. The moon lighting our way back to the huts.

"Have you got a padlock, Chloe?" Jim asks me now.

"Yes, but I didn't use it last night, not up here."

"Do me a favour then and put it on tonight, will you? Better to be safe. You don't want your money or passport stolen."

Can't really see why I should but I do as I am told and have to be content with the moon shining through the small window instead of streaming through the open door. There is no water tonight but who cares when you are 7,500 metres in the sky with birdsong, flowers and fabulous views?

Huge vampire bats fly like vultures and make a strange noise. Men carry parrots, finches, ducks and chickens in wire baskets attached to a yoke across their shoulders. Even the bobbing head of a small child, so safely contained in her round metal carrycot. Back in Kathmandu I explore the streets and in between make fruitless and frustrating visits to the bank and endless phone calls to the U Go Overland office, which no longer replies. Huge disappointment fills me and anger, too, and a sense of foolishness. By coincidence, Jim seems to be staying in the same small guesthouse so we meet each evening and sometimes bump into each other during one or other sightseeing trip. Of the Crab Man I still say nothing, but increasingly he is taking up my every thought. Each night, after tucking Rosie's picture and the broken butterfly necklace under my pillow, his face swims into my sight and I feel that prickling sensation up my spine, remembering nothing until the next morning, when I awake refreshed and energised. Every morning the urge to go back is greater. I need to explore these new but not unpleasant sensations. Find out what's what.

But for today, while I still wait, I have a choice between having my forehead anointed with red rice grains by the King, attending a ritual killing and drinking blood in Durbar Square, joining a motley band, or following a craven image of a God as it wavers its way along the streets. I decide instead to eat a yak cheese sandwich and a disinfected salad with Jim before visiting the Tibetan Buddhist Centre. Tomorrow I shall visit the Kumari, that five-year-old child chosen to represent the pure living Goddess. So many new Goddesses I have been introduced to! I like the idea of them. Along one of the small streets is a bookstore and there I see a book all about finding the hidden goddess within ourselves. A voluptuous Botticelli-type figure reclines on the cover. That's good. Us goddesses are obviously allowed to spread a little – in fact it's an essential prerequisite! Whoever invented 'love handles' obviously knew his stuff. Now, why should I think it was a male? "Goddesses' bodies are bodies that truly know love in all her aspects." That's good, then. No need to worry if my slimmed down version, grown gaunt from the heat, gets back into full bloom. I put the book back and finally find one on the myths behind the many Tibetan and Hindu Goddesses.

The little Kumari has to undergo rigorous tests to prove her fearlessness, before she is taken from her family and kept in an ornately carved wooden house in Durbar Square. Never to shed blood, she is carried everywhere and rarely appears in public, though she is sometimes held up at a window. It is from outside this window that I shall see her, watched over and held by her minders. On the day she menstruates or cuts herself, she will be handed back to her family and the process of selection will begin all over again. What a strange pre-destined life is this?

The first pangs of stomach ache hit me that evening and the next three days are spent in the bathroom either heaving or sitting. Embarrassingly, Jim calls by twice a day with fresh water and tablets bought off the roadside medical stall. Nice to know he's around if I should need serious help and good to get the tablets, but otherwise my real need is to be left in private. Looking at the crumbled packet in my hand, I wonder if these are secondhand and out-of-date medicines but I swallow them just the same.

I make one last futile attempt to reach Claude and the office before I feel well enough to fly out and on to Calcutta,

Jim insisting on accompanying me to the airport, where he shakes my hand. "Are you sure you feel well enough, Chloe? Good luck. Hope to see you again one day." He tucks the piece of paper with my New York phone number into his pocket and waits until I go through to the departure lounge.

Calcutta at two in the morning is no place for anyone, not even a 'growing through going' woman! The airport is empty, I can't change my travellers' cheques, so I have no Indian money and all tourist taxis have stopped. By the time I have persuaded the bored acting manager to trust me and exchange me some money, I am almost the only person left in this bleak concrete building. A particularly unpleasant looking man moves closer and watches as I stuff the notes into my neck purse.

"Please leave me alone. I don't need your help." A nearby policeman doesn't help either. "Ask this man to leave me alone, please." He pretends not to understand and doesn't bother to reply.

Wearing a confidence I don't feel, I hitch my backpack onto my shoulders and make for the exit. Just a line of yellow taxis, parked for the night. I have rung and prebooked a room in a well-known old tea house but now I am not even sure it will be open should I be able to get there.

"Look, madam. You need taxi. I have taxi. I take you." The unpleasant one is still attached to me. Still trying to attract my attention. I am tired. My guts still ache.

"You have a tourist taxi? A yellow taxi?"

"Yes, lady. I show you." And he runs off into the darkness. Now, in the overhead lights outside, I watch several men saunter towards me.

"You like money changed?"

"I take you to a hotel, madam."

Is this a rerun of my arrival? Suddenly, I wish it were Singh here. All the other passengers have left hours ago, it seems, and there is no one else to turn to. As the taxi draws up beside me, I know I only have two choices. Spend the night here or go with the unknown. Neither is an attractive proposition, but I do have a reservation. As the clutch of men surround me, my driver pulls up, jumps out and tugs at my bag. Just in time, I remember to agree a price. As I get in, I insist, "Are you sure this really is your own taxi?"

"Oh yes, madam."

Two more men jump in. One beside me and the other next to the driver. In that same moment I am out and back on the tarmac. "No way! I am *not* travelling with three of you. Forget it!" Picking my bag up, I turn back towards the airport building.

A quick unintelligible conversation and the other two back off. "Come, lady. You quite safe."

Please God let it be safe! I get back in, give him the address and away we go. Less than five minutes along the road, he pulls up and turns around. "Madam. This is no ordinary taxi."

"What!" Anger and fear make me shout at him. Disbelief, tears of frustration and tiredness all well up. "We agreed a price! What do you mean?"

And so begins a living nightmare as my driver drives me around the outskirts of Calcutta for over an hour. Sometimes he stops, gets out and leaves me, always demanding that I either pay him large sums of money or at least agree to him taking me to the hotel of his choice. My voice grows weaker and wearier as we argue and shout at each other. Sometimes we seem to be crossing derelict building sites, sometimes passing through whole villages of drunken men. As they leer up against the windows, their hands pressed against the glass, I cower in the back, the penknife Spotty had insisted upon open in my hand.

"Are you a Hindu?"

"Of course, lady."

"Then why are you doing this? Take me to where I want to go. I have a reservation."

"It very late now, madam. No place is open."

"Never mind. Just take me there." And yet once more he leaves me. He leaves the door swinging and saunters off into the shadows. I can just see him in a dark huddle on a distant corner. We seem to be parked on vast wasteland.

"Don't leave me here. Come back. Please!" I am almost bleating. I forget Jean Brodie, forget everything in the darkness of the night. I feel afraid, alone and vulnerable.

At around 4am he gives in and we pull up outside large metal gates with what seems like nothing behind them. One final rush of energy propels me out of the taxi door and onto the street, my bag dragging behind me.

"You see, madam, it is too late. It is closed. I told you. Now you have to come with me." Triumph gives his voice added strength as he leans towards me to take my bag a second time.

"Oh, I'm sure there must be a bell somewhere here," I mutter, fighting for time and trying to appear cool as I claw at the railings desperately searching for a bell. In the distance I can just make out the shape of a long low building. By now my voice is just a thread.

The fact that I am tired, unwell, makes me unusually weak and scared. The now not unexpected throng of ragged, drunken men appears out of the darkness to crowd me against the metal of the gates when, like music, I hear the voice of an angel close to my left ear

"Let me help you. What is the problem?" A tall upright man, all in white, has pushed through the small crowd and is now beside me. I explain and then watch as he cups his hands together and makes dove 'cooing' noises, blowing the sound through the gates. The others all back off. How this slight sound is going to help I do not know and can hardly believe it when an old man walks slowly towards me from the other side. Quietly and in perfect English my angel explains my reservation, the gates are opened and I am through. They clang shut and are locked behind me. The faces of the men press up against them.

You should always thank an angel, Chloe. Remembering, I turn back. "Thank you for helping me. I don't know who you are but you saved me from a very difficult situation." Raising my eyes to his I find that his eyes are eyes to drown in and the lustrous dark hair falling in waves to his shoulders frames that face of beauty and love. A face that is now so familiar to me. The Crab Man! I have to stop myself from swooning and, hitching my bag onto my shoulders, I turn and run towards the Tea House.

By 7am I am standing beside the reception desk. "Please order me a taxi to the airport. I am flying out today." The taxi, when it comes, takes me to the airport within ten minutes. Three hours later I am on the plane. Going back to Delhi.

Chapter 9

The coach crawls slowly through Chadni Chowk towards the mosque. Returning so soon brings with it a feeling of the surreal, adding a dreamlike quality to our winding course. Nothing's changed here. And yet I feel as if everything has changed. The road, just as congested as before, the teeming mass of humanity flooding the narrow street in just the same way. We pass the same stalls, hear the same cries and watch as the same goats, dicing again with death, dodge through the traffic. As we approach the mosque, I am already on my feet.

"Careful, madam." He puts out a tentative hand to steady me and hold me back. The guide is not the same, though. A much fatter man, the buttons of his crisp white shirt straining across his round belly where it tucks into his neat grey slacks. A cheap gold watch around his hairless and small wrist. His feet encased in what looks like a new pair of shiny, brown open-toed sandals, now making their way towards the door. A quickening inside of me, like an unborn baby, and then I am right behind him. My nervous anticipation heightened, my mouth dry with the foretaste.

"Please wait for me, madam. I will help you all through."
But I don't want helping through. I am not going to go up
those broad steps or to sit in the shade like the last time. A
sudden flash of Sean's face as he ducked through the low
door in the mosque courtyard comes back into my mind and
just for a second I wonder how he is. Where he is.

The guide climbs down and holds both his arms
outstretched, shielding us from the line of beggars who now
press forward. "Don't be long now, please. Back here in
forty minutes." Well, I doubt it!

Ducking under his arm, I hurry away from him and
disappear into the crowd. His voice calling after me is quickly
lost among the cacophony of the many street sounds. To
gain time, I cross over to a stall selling bales of old cloth,
joining the other buyers as I run my hands through the pile
of smaller pieces piled high on the old trestle tabletop. Next
to me, an English woman is haggling over the price of faded
blue cotton covered with tiny intricate embroidery and blue
beading. Thankfully the seller is far too busy for the moment
to pay any attention to me. Feigning interest in the fine but
grubby lilac lawn, with its wandering pattern of green vine-
shaped leaves, I take a look back towards the mosque.

"Please, lady." The nudge on the arm is from the one
good hand of a leper holding a dirty polystyrene cup. The
white bandaged stump of the other is giving off a terrible
rotting smell. The stallholder rushes around the table, gabbles
dismissively, shooing him away with his hands. "So sorry,
madam." Another burst of angry words and the poor old
man wanders off to tap the elbow of another tourist. Again,
I glance towards the mosque. A whole group of beggars
huddle together but however much I crane my neck, I just

cannot find the small crouched figure among them. As another coach lumbers slowly up they move forward as one body but there are no slow shuffling crablike movements, no arresting face or tumbling black hair that I can see. Please God! He *has* to be here somewhere! He *must* be! Could he be on the other side of the steps? Horns toot, cars swerve and I dodge but I make it and lean against the wall of a crumbling old building on the other side. If I pull my shawl well over my face I can stand back, hidden in its long shadow and watch, my eyes fixed on those steps and the twenty or so beggars who wait for the tourist buses that arrive and leave at regular short intervals. I see my guide scanning the crowd but I make no move forward towards him. Finally, shrugging, he climbs on board; the coach turns and starts making its slow way back without me.

Hours later, I am still watching when the beggars move away, disperse and disappear into the gathering darkness. Without my noticing, dusk has fallen. It's around about this time too that I realise I have been half holding my breath and have to make myself take deep gulps of air. I am also suddenly very hungry and overwhelmed with tiredness. The disappointment at not seeing the Crab Man brings all those feelings that belong with dejection. Dispiritedness. Now I know it's sort of when the spirit fades a bit. The light dims. A kind of letdown feeling after all the enthusiasm that has brought me back here. Who is this man who can appear before me, fill my dreams? Becomes my angel when I need one? Even make me faint onto the tomb of Mumtaz? The craving to know gnaws away inside of me. *But Chloe, it was never going to be easy. And what are you going to say to him when you do find him?* I shall just keep trying, that's all. But I feel deeply disappointed as I take the nearest rickshaw and go back to the hostel and a restless night, his face constantly waking me just as I am ready to drift into sleep.

Up with the dawn and too early for everything, so I sit and wait in the reception area. Sunlight floods the marble floor and sounds of doors bang as people make their way to the showers or push through the swing doors into the eating hall. I have on my cream Punjabi suit with the green silk shawl across my shoulders, its soft-fringed ends hanging down my back. In my pocket lies the broken butterfly but apart from that hidden adornment, my fingers are ringless, my throat and earlobes bare. My mind completely taken up with considering what today will bring.

"May I?" The voice sounds familiar all right.

"Jim! What on earth are you doing here?" When he had waved me off to Calcutta he hadn't given any indication that he would be flying out to Delhi so soon. A very serious looking Jim. Why, his expression is almost stern. Since I last saw him his pleasant-looking face has become more tanned, which colour contrasts with the cornflower blue shirt very agreeably. His horn-rimmed spectacles hang on a cord around his neck just below the open neck of the shirt. Just now, the girl in the yellow sari is gesturing across to those of us waiting that the coach is arriving and I get up just as he sits down beside me.

"I didn't know you were coming to Delhi! I'm so sorry Jim, but I haven't time to talk. I have to go. Are you staying here? Maybe tonight?" Then, seeing the look of concern that crosses his face, I add, "Is everything all right?"

"I'm afraid I'll have to ask you not to go anywhere, Chloe. I need to talk to you. Please come with me." And he puts his hand under my elbow to steer me towards the dining room.

"Jim, I'm really sorry but I can't right now. I'm meant to be on that coach. Can't we do this later on?" Agitation making my voice sharper and high pitched. "I have something really important that I have to do today. Can't whatever it is wait?"

With his free hand, he pulls a blue card out of the pocket of his short-sleeved shirt and holds it out towards me. A small plasticised card. About two inches long. A bit like a calling card, perhaps, is the bizarre thought that flits across my mind. But calling cards didn't have your name and rank on them, did they? The size of a business card, it feels sharp edged and smooth surfaced with a photograph of Jim Lawley, CID, East Sussex Police…

"Madam, the coach is going without you." I nod vaguely at her through a fog. Something terrible must have happened! My mother? Rosie? Not Rosie! Please let it not be Rosie. I could never survive anything happening to Rosie. Never. I don't dare to look up at him. In spite of the warmth, it's suddenly so cold. My legs feel like they might give way underneath me.

"Take it easy, Chloe," he says gently and pushes me down into a chair at a discreet corner table. "I'll get you some tea."

"Who is it? Please tell me quickly. I have to know but I don't know whether I'll be able to bear it."

"It's Sean, Chloe, and U Go Overland." Then. seeing my face, which feels like its drained of all its colour: "Sorry. I didn't mean to break it to you like that. You've been proving a little difficult to keep up with, what with your swift turnaround and changes of destination. I couldn't let you disappear off again. Besides, it's costing a fortune in airfares!" His grin lightens the mood as he pats my arm and then goes off to get the tea.

A cup of tea in front of us both, he leans back. His face softens and he speaks gently to me. "I need to ask you some questions, Chloe. Fortunately, I think we can safely say that we've established that you are not implicated. Naive or nice, perhaps; foolish maybe, but innocent."

Innocent? Implicated? "Implicated in what? Are you sure this can't wait till this evening?" With the relief that Rosie is safe, the frustration is coming back. Frustration at having my plans upset again. It will now be yet *another* day before I can talk to the Crab Man. Now that I have established that it's not anything to do with Rosie that brings him here, my desire to get to the Crab Man is greater than my curiosity to know what Jim is talking about.

For the next two hours I listen as Jim talks. It seems that even before the trip started, Sean and U Go Overland were under surveillance. Remembering the brown paper package, my body goes from cold to red hot, like a hot flash all over. Money "for repairs on the bus", Sean had said.

"Sean was arrested on arrival at Gatwick Airport and by now James and Claude will have joined him in custody in Lewes Prison. The bus is cordoned off and guarded for the moment while Forensic go over it. We have found a kilo of heroin under the back passenger seat and traces of much more. Sean knew his days were numbered and was losing his nerve. Panicked. Used you as a decoy. That's why he stopped and took others along, too. Trying to make us think he really had stopped his part in their drug-trafficking game.

Over the years these trips have moved drugs not only around India but also back into England on a regular basis. Fortunately for you, we have been able to eliminate you from our enquiries. Sean has made a statement admitting everything; that he deliberately duped you and that you had no idea of what was really going on, but you'll have to make a statement yourself. James has also admitted that you were just an innocent passenger. With luck we can keep you out of it. I'm afraid quite a lot of people are going to be arrested."

I think of Hari Harsh then. His slave proposal, his drunkenness and unwashed state and his kindness in taking me to the Taj. I think of all the other men who greeted Sean nearly everywhere we went. I think of Sean. That hurts a bit. Makes me feel a bit of a fool. Being so trusting, so taken in.

Later Jim takes me through my statement. "We'll sign and witness it tonight when the others are here. For now you look deadbeat." A simple and, yes, innocent account of my trip on the clapped-out old bus. A magical trip. Only I couldn't put that. Jim would never have understood and the receiver of the statement would probably think I was taking something I shouldn't!

"I think I'd like to go back to my room now." My mind so full that I don't pick up on "the others" bit. It is too late to go to the mosque and I do feel completely drained.

"Of course. Why don't we have dinner later?" He puts his arm lightly around my shoulders and gives me a sort of gentle squeeze.

"I suppose so," I say, but that sounds ungracious so I try to make up by forcing a tired smile before slowly taking the stairs. My aching head reels with thousands more questions to be asked and answered. I am not quite sure I can grasp it all. I think back to that night in the kitchen in New York when I told Rosie and Jeannie where I was going. In my wildest dreams I could never have envisaged a trip like this.

The repeated knocking pulls me out of the heavy stupor, my head fuzzy with amazement. "Miss Chloe? Are you there? *Yoo hoo!* Miss Chloe?" And there she is! Pounding on my door! Can I believe this? All wobbling chins and lavender-smelling, in her favourite purple. A Punjabi suit and folded shawl with embroidered pink flowers gathered together and over one shoulder. Long exotic earrings of something that looks like amethyst but surely can't be, hang from her ears. The usual armful of glass bangles jangling and almost matching the purple nail varnish. "Good to see you again, Miss Chloe!" And once again I am back in those damp folds.

Linking her arm through mine, she leads me, quite speechless, downstairs. Once in the foyer, she marches me up to a very small and wizened old man. His face like old, creased parchment as he smiles, his beady eyes bright and deep. His moustache smart and clipped close. His cream linen suit sporting an immaculate white handkerchief, folded and peeping out of the top pocket. What my father would have called "a dapper little man", which always seemed to me to be ever so slightly damning. The emphasis being on the little, I suppose.

"Allow me to introduce you to my husband, Gopal." Edna pushes me forward. "It means Lord Krishna, you know." She says this last bit with pride. Lord Krishna now joins his palms and bows towards me. "*Namaste.*"

Jim chooses this moment to stroll in through the outside

door and joins us, shaking hands with Gopal and kissing Edna on each cheek. So they know each other? I try hard to change the foolish but fixed expression I feel sure my face is now permanently wearing, and wonder how many shocks my heart can sustain in one day.

The restaurant is discreet and dark and full of framed black and white photographs of members of the owner's family, presumably. In one, a small child in school uniform, clutching a bag, stares fixedly and very solemnly into the camera. Another is a family group, all gleaming white teeth beaming into the camera. The tablecloths are starched, the napkins crisp, the silver polished. I am barely coherent and have little appetite but another whiff of Edna's lavender perfume prompts me to open my bum bag, scrabble around and pull out the small phial of lavender I found under the bus seat and hand it back to her.

"Oh my! Fancy my leaving that behind! How careless of me. Why, I'll never be employed again." And she turns towards Jim, giving him a large wink.

Employed? I am not sure what she is talking about, in fact, I am not at all sure I understand anything any more.

"Honey, you are one courageous woman. Fancy driving the bus like that. Don't you think she's courageous, my beloved?" She turns towards Gopal. He pats her hand, which today bears a ring on each finger. "Well, Chloe, when I told you that I came here forty-five years ago it wasn't a lie, but I didn't come back because I never ever left in the first place. Gopal and I have been together ever since. Haven't we, my sweet Gopee?" And she looks at him again, leans forward and plants a kiss on top of his small, balding head, leaving behind a bow shaped ring of bright pink lipstick. He looks up at her quite adoringly. He so small and neat and she so enormous and overflowing. "We married, you know. We live in Kashi. Oh, you might call that Varanasi or Benares. Gopal's family has a shop selling brassware. He used to work for the police." The police bit hisses across the table in a loud stage whisper and then – with a coquettish glance towards Jim - "Still does sometimes. Gopee and I have been keeping an eye on the Kashi end of things." *The swishing hips disappearing into the dark shop, the laugh.* So, Jim and Edna and Gopal have all been working together?

I don't think Lord Krishna and I say more than half a dozen words between us all through the meal, Jim and Edna holding the stage until we all walk back to the hostel together, Edna coming up to my room to see me safely in. Before I let her go there is something I have to know. "Edna, all that stuff with the crystal ball, was that true?" Immediately she is in my room, the door closed swiftly behind her. "You'll never guess who came the other night. Cary Grant! Sat on the edge of the bathtub. Such a nice chat we had. You know, dear, Sean never was the man for you. I did try to warn you but we had to keep you travelling, you see." No point trying to explain that it wasn't Sean I was interested in. I wonder what her crystal ball would say about the Crab Man?

She bends to kiss me goodnight and I remember something else. "That smell of lavender in the room in Rewa, was that you too?"

"Just had to check your room. Found a packet under the mattress of the dirty bed. Leaving the bed dirty is one good way of making sure no one gets in it." And throwing her head back she laughs, a deep-throated, full sound. "A good hiding place. Course I didn't take the packet, didn't want to give the game away. Let's talk more tomorrow. Sleep tight, honey. You look beat." And she sashays out, closing the door behind her.

At last I am alone and can collapse again. My head, still buzzing with the day's events, feels like I am wearing a tight hat. Before I go to sleep I remember to scribble a note for Jim telling him I shall be away tomorrow. Then I put Rosie's photo under my pillow along with the butterfly, set my alarm clock and fall into bed and pray for the Crab Man to come to me in my dreams.

My taxi deposits me at the mosque steps and I cross quickly towards the same old building where I have to wait half an hour before they start to arrive, close against the wall as the chaos of daily life moves around me, its pace relentless. From all directions they come, limping, on crutches, one man is even wheeled in on a kind of trolley and deposited at the steps all in a heap. Taking a deep breath, I pluck up courage and go towards them.

"Please can you tell me where I can find the man who wears the wooden sabots on his hands?" I direct my question to a young man, the old wooden crutch under his arm, and one eye white blind. He doesn't appear to hear or understand me. Is he deaf too? Asking for alms, they start clutching at me with dirty hands.

"No. Please *Listen* to me. *Where is he*?" But they don't want to know. The man on the trolley has no legs, just stumps where his knees would be. He gives me a toothless grin and holds out one hand in supplication, palm upwards. The other hand can't be seen – its arm too having been cut off at the elbow or rotted and dropped off.

As they press closer my voice rises. "The man with the sabots. He was here with you all. I saw him only a few weeks ago. You *must* know him. You must know who he is." I try again. But it's useless. "Please, lady, you kind lady!" My shawl gets tugged at yet again and I feel it slip from my head.

"Why won't you listen to me? It's important to me!" I feel I want to cry with exasperation. It's no good. I shall have to find someone else to ask. Twisting my body, turning, I trip over someone's dirty bare foot and fall down onto the road and into a sea of moving bodies, my ankle twisted underneath me. Cowering in the dirt, covering my head with my arms I wait to be trampled upon as they pack even more closely around me. With my face so close to the ground the smell is overpowering. Not just feet and weeping leprosy but dirty bodies, drains and urine and faeces. Dirt and dust and dung all around me. (This is the level at which *he* spends his whole day. Looking at the ants and blow flies and every other sort of crawling insect that lives by eating filth.)

"Come, madam. You want taxi? I have very good taxi. Very clean." A slim brown hand comes down and along with some others helps me to my feet.

I can't help it, I start to laugh in spite of my throbbing ankle. "I don't believe this. Just help me up will you, Singh? And no, I don't want a taxi but I *do* need your help."

He draws himself up tall, flushed with importance. "Stand back, please. This very fine lady. American." His voice is authoritative and the beggars drop back a bit and a space is cleared. Lots of hands are helping me now and then Singh and I push our way slowly through the small crowd towards a shop and enter its dark interior, where a chair is brought forward for me to sit on. Singh issues instructions. "This is my niece," he says as a shy young girl comes somewhere from the back and lights a small primus stove, setting a pan of water to boil. Soon a hot glass is in my hands and my ankle and foot are sitting in a bucket of cold water. All around the dark walls are rough shelves filled with cheap kitchen utensils and pots and pans and stainless steel jugs and bowls. Piles of scissors of all sizes and various brushes and implements used for gardening. Was it only yesterday I passed four men cutting a small square of grass in a municipal park? All of them using large scissors whilst the overseer stood under a tree, leaning against the trunk, smoking a *beedi* – that strange brand of slim Indian cigarette made from leaves and little tobacco.

"Singh, you do turn up at the oddest moments. What are you doing here?"

"Lady, you should not be out all alone like this. I keep an eye on you since you come to Delhi. What you need is a good husband to look after you." Now I come to think of it I do seem to have caught sight of him daily, usually loitering around the hostel gate.

"Not now, Singh, please but you *can* help me. I am looking for someone. That man who was here a few weeks ago on the mosque steps. The one with the wooden sabots on his hands. The man who can only crawl along the ground. You *must* know him. Please try and think Singh. It's very important."

His face looks suddenly grave (or could it be sad?) as he bows his head towards his bare feet with the two missing toes.

"You mean Baba, madam. Baba's dead."

"No! Please. Don't say that." I don't want to hear that.

"*No*. Not that." Disbelief, anger and then a feeling of being cheated all roll through me. "But when? I saw him only a few weeks ago. He *can't* be dead"

"It was an accident. He was knocked over."

As his words sink in, I put my head upon my knees and abandon myself to a sudden feeling of utter hopelessness. Entering the long familiar tunnel of grief once again, the dark night of the soul comes swiftly and drops her cloak around me. The Crab Man held the key to a doorway. Now I shall never know what is on the other side.

How long I remain like that I cannot say but then I recognise a light touch upon my shoulder. The man is very old but his eyes are kind and a clear light blue.

"Come," is all he says and I know that I will go with him.

The room is small and white and bare except for the many books on the shelves lining the walls from floor to ceiling. There is a screen across one corner behind which I can see a few kitchen utensils all neatly arranged upon a table. A curtain falls across an alcove and a mat is neatly rolled up on the floor. Deep peace and stillness live in these four walls and, in the air, a faint smell of sandalwood incense. The only light coming from the candle in the iron sconce upon the wall. Unrolling the mat, he invites me to sit. "You ask for Baba?"

I can only nod.

"Did you have questions you wanted to ask him?" His voice is low and sweet and melodious as he settles himself cross-legged on the other side and opposite to me.

When I find my voice it is small, like a child's. Barely above a whisper. "Who was he?" I can't look at him but keep my head bowed.

"Tell me, when you looked at Baba, what did you see?"

"A beautiful man." And now I do look up and at him with the strength of my repeated words. "Truly beautiful."

"And when Baba looked at you what did you feel?"

"I felt as if he *really* saw me. Beyond the external me…"

Now he nods his head very slowly. Then, almost to himself he says, "Ah, I see. You stepped out of the mould. You saw Baba and he saw you."

What riddles are these?

The old man continues. "You are in Baba and Baba is in you. For always. You see, Baba's body may be dead but he lives for ever." Getting up, he takes a book down and opens it at a page marked with a strip of frayed, red material. "That which is beyond this world is without form and without suffering. Those who know that become immortal." He shuts the book "Shvetashvatara Upanishad." All completely double-Dutch to me.

"You see, you reached out to Baba and he in turn reaches out to you. The seed was dormant, now it lives. It's woken up."

Changing the subject suddenly, he continues. "Is this the first time you travel to India?"

I find myself telling him everything. Even my "Growing through Going" slogan, which now seems so trite. He doesn't laugh at me. He makes me fragrant tea and hands me a bowl of thick sweet rice flavoured with cardamom. Much later he leads me across to the curtained alcove and gestures to the low wooden bed with its huge pile of cushions heaped at one end. "You need to sleep now. You will be safe here."

The nest of cushions cradles me as I drift off to the sound

of soft movements from the other side of the curtain. With the morning comes a quiet voice – "May I?" – and a cup of tea comes through the curtain. "Take your time. There is no hurry."

Well, I sure do take my time. Nearly a week I stay with the old man. He never makes me feel a nuisance. Is always patient with me. By day I read, think much, and rest my ankle, peacefully propped up against the many deep cushions. We don't speak. Taking a peep from between the curtains across my bed, I sometimes see him performing Yoga postures on the rolled out mat, but mostly he is still and sitting in the lotus position. An expression of what I can only describe as deep serenity upon his gentle face or is it what you call bliss?

In the evenings we sit together cross-legged on the mat, the candle spluttering, and I listen to his quiet voice, absorb his wise words. Many books are taken down, passages selected to be discussed and pondered upon. Questions I need to ask. And words. Poems. That epic poem, the Bhagavad-Gita. Lines to remember. "It is both near and far, both within and without every creature; it moves and is unmoving". Each night I fall into a deep sleep. The quiet words of the old man comforting my ears and following me into my dreams. Twice, in that week, I awake in the night to sit bolt upright as a voice calls, "Neerja, little Neerja", but when I look around the curtain of the bed there is no one there. The old man remains straight and motionless upon the mat.

As the days pass I begin the struggle to understand the difference between self and ego, soul, Brahma and the cosmic union with Brahman, the Godhead.

"You see everything comes back to the self. When you enquire into the self then you realise you are everything but you are also nothing. If you are everything then you are also a part of Baba, of everyone, the whole universe. Baba *is* you."

We spend one evening of delight discussing the many *samskaras*, those Hindu practises designed to guide the individual through the various stages of life; the naming ceremony of a child, the *mundan* or shaving of the head ceremony, the marriage ceremony, the ceremony of *garbhadhana* which takes place at conception and the worship ritual on the death of the body. I can see those burning bodies at the Ghats in Kashi, smell the oil, the woodsmoke, the incense. "First we bathe the body then we cover it with sandalwood paste and decorate it with sweet flowers, sprinkling gold dust upon the face and head. Twigs are lit, prayers spoken and the mouth of the departed touched with the kindling. On death we honour the body that has been our temple but we discard it like old clothes. There is no further use for it."

Later, after a bowl of rice and vegetables flavoured with spices, he tells me: "This is a spiritual journey you are making, Chloe, human life, a school of learning. When you meet pain or sorrow along the way you can choose to see it as an opportunity or as just another blow. Turn inwards, get stuck and live with self-pity, or turn outwards and grow forward." I had told him about Mike and about my childhood of clipped wings. He senses the deep hole inside. Sees the pain.

He tells me of the four yogas or paths of Hindu Mysticism; we talk together of the concept of *shraddha*, of the heart, and of the *samsara,* the eternal circle of birth and death. "When the self gets weak, then the breaths gather around him. When the person in the eye turns away then he takes to himself those particles of light and descends into the heart, becomes non-knowing of forms, or *upanishads*."

"I think I understand. You mean there is always existence. It's continuous?"

"It is very simple. The living are on one side of the piece of paper and those without form are on the other side but it is still the same, one piece of paper." And his sweet smile falls upon me.

Slowly what seemed like riddles become clearer. Karma, sower and reaper, action and the result of action. Then the whole idea of reincarnation. So much to think upon.

"Just keep swimming the ocean, Chloe. Go for the horizon. Don't look towards the shore for rescue. Don't be distracted. Keep going. Keep growing." And we laugh quietly together. "Fill your own heart until it overflows, then let the stream touch all who pass by you."

A key turns, a door opens. Just a crack, and then a bit more as I digest the profound truths offered to me. Slowly a clarity dawns. How I make this human journey is suddenly of the utmost significance. "Don't pay attention to others who would try to divert you and always be true to yourself. Trust your intuition. You will travel well."

The last night he comes towards me with a parcel wrapped in newspaper. "This is for you. Please to open it." The paper falls away and inside is a pair of wooden sabots, the leather where his hands have rubbed it all thin and shiny, the wooden soles worn away from the constant pressure of his hands as he crawled along the ground.

"You see, Baba was my son. My gift from God. When he was born, my wife and I named him Duranjaya, our Heroic Son. He brought great joy to everyone who knew him. So wise that soon everyone called him Baba or Father. So compassionate that everyone loved him. When he died, he was taken and cremated and his ashes scattered on the water of the Ganga."

Running my hands over the worn leather, I see again that face, those deep burning eyes boring into mine. The tiny bottom sticking up in the air, the stick legs and calloused feet, the big muscled chest and arms.

"Little Neerja is what he called you. Lotus Flower."

Can I have heard right? "I'm sorry, I don't think I understand."

"The day you saw Baba he told me about you. He called you Lotus Flower because he knew the seed had taken root, would grow into a bud and then a beautiful blossom. So now you can always find him inside yourself, always call upon him. He will watch over you. You are watching over each other. You are watching over yourself." No longer riddles but a revelation of a truth which I find deep inside of myself.

So! I have been living in Baba's house, sleeping in Baba's bed. That huge pile of cushions to support his poor top-heavy and twisted body. Although I hardly dared believe it, deep down I sort of really knew. Such tranquil days and nights among the soft cushions. Profoundly moved, reaching into my pocket, I take out the broken butterfly necklace and put it into his hand. "I am letting go of this. I want you to have it."

"Ah! The butterfly of transformation, Chloe. First an egg, then larva, then cocoon, and finally the birth of the beautiful butterfly, you see? A life's journeying, Chloe. It is just beginning. Keep searching. Keep enquiring. And always remember that the way in which you looked at Baba is the clue to the way in which he looked at you. Beyond each other's outward appearances. When you can master that then you meet each other on another plain."

My heart full, I can hardly bear to tear myself away from this gentle man who has somehow given me back to myself. I know it is no coincidence but fate, and Baba, who brought me to him. I no longer feel cheated by Baba dying because I *feel* his love inside of myself and, in these last moments talking with his father, I make a discovery. I also love myself. That small innocent child who still lives inside of me is really quite lovable. I think of the strait jacket that came with my birth and know now that I have always had the ability within myself to throw it off. It's just taken a long time, that's all. But I finally made it. I want to sing, shout, jump up and down, swing around lampposts. Tell the whole world how I am feeling!

"You will find me on the banks of the Ganga. My Heroic Son has no need of me now. I shall be waiting there." Waiting beside that great flowing Goddess until the death of the body. Until "the breaths gather around". Until he takes unto himself "those particles of light and descends into the heart". His beautiful smile, so sweet and gentle, as he bows and once more wishes me "*Namaste. Om Shanti.* Peace."

It is with immense inner peace that I regretfully leave

him and climb into the taxi. I wave until I can no longer see him.

Jim is still waiting, a bit cross, but Singh had been sent to find him and tell him I would be away for a few days. The old man had thought of everything. Everywhere I go I see people smiling, a permanent grin glued to my face. Like a butterfly, I swoop laughing here and there, shopping till I drop in the bazaar, weighed down with presents to take home, as Mr Raj and I laugh together. Staggering from his underground heaven loaded down by bags of silks, shawls of every hue and simple white cotton drawstring trousers, I make my way back to the hostel. Joy my constant companion. When I go to bed at night, my heart sings. I think of Baba, of the old man and feel warm and inspired. I can only wonder, with great gratitude, at their touching upon my life. A flame has been lit that can never go out. Then again, I know that the flame is always alight inside each of us just waiting to be fanned. Thinking back to that smooth and polished exterior I am so glad that it can never be put together again. Life inside a cage was such a stifling experience. How can a spirit soar when reined back by the barriers of conventional thinking? A bird fly with clipped wings?

The sabots sit beside my bed. I run my hands again and again over the indentations almost with disbelief. A monster? A freak of nature or of God? I no longer have to look for the answer.

I buy books and read till dawn breaks. I put in calls to Bob and my mother. I visit the Rajghat, breathe deeply of the frangipani trees and the perfume from the millions of strewn petals as I stare at the simple platform where the remains of Gandhi were cremated. The music of the fountains playing in the background. What was it Gandhi said? "Freedom is like a birth. Until we are fully free we are slaves". Yes, this journey has been a birth process – at times confusing – but finally bringing me to this place of freedom. From which I can never turn back. Not until that day in the future when the "breaths come" and I return to the heart. No longer a slave to someone else's standards or ideals. Someone else's dreams. No longer bound by the boundaries of someone else's agenda. I buy a postcard picture of the Half Naked Fakir and resolve not to send it to anyone but to keep it and so remind me to always be myself. Always expressing my own personality. Always allowing that stream of love to flow towards others rhythmically back and forth like the tides. Always seeing beyond the outward appearance. Meeting each other on other sunnier plains. The free spirit flying beyond all boundaries, finding no barriers on its journey to the sun.

A last meal with Jim and then Singh is there to take me to the airport. Dear Singh. He has been a constant feature of my trip. Now he tries one more time. "Are you sure, lady? I have good job. Good husband material. I think you need good man to look after you." If it wouldn't give him the wrong idea, I would kiss him. What would I have done without him? Singh, too, played a leading part in my journey of the soul. After all, it was Singh who called the old man. Singh who was there the moment I landed at the airport. Singh who was always lingering around the hostel gate, keeping an eye out for me.

"Oh Singh! I have to go and find my daughter but I feel

very honoured by all your proposals and I do hope that you find a good wife. By the way, Singh, that old man you took me to. Baba's father. I don't know his name."

"Markandeya."

"What does that mean?"

"It means he is a wise man, lady."

All too soon I am on the plane that will fly me direct to New York. My overflowing bags of ridiculous clothes, left at my mothers in Lincoln, can stay there. Rosie will be back in a week and I want to be there to meet her. I can barely contain my excitement with the thought of all the sharing we are going to do. The seat next to me is empty until the last moment. "Hello, Chloe."

Not again! "Jim! What on earth are you doing here?" I say as he slides in beside me. "Not more bad news?"

"Taken a week's leave to see you safely back to New York." He says it quite seriously but I start to laugh. After the journey I have made these last few months, this trip back to New York seems like a piece of cake!

"There's no knowing where you'll end up! Thought you'd better have an escort!"

There is something I want to ask him, too. "You don't have an Australian accent!"

"Yes. Well, that was just a blind. Had to think of some way of getting in there. Fancied trying the Australian tourist."

He leans back and closes his eyes, spectacles slipping down his nose, as the plane skims down the runway and launches into the air. I shut my eyes too, and immediately see that arresting face, that tumbling black hair, those deep eyes to get lost in.

"Little Neerja." And he is standing there beside me. That look of love. My heart fills up. I smile a secret smile that I will smile for the rest of my life. It lives inside of me. *Namaste. Om Shanti.* Peace.

Postscript
CAPE MAY
Three years on

I am writing this seated on the pink button back chair in the same room, the same pink satin bedspread upon the bed, the repro furniture. Same seashore views. Stefan still the mother hen. I, too, am the same but not the same. No longer the woman filled with grief and self pity. I truly have moved on. I see life now through different eyes. New spectacles.

A month after I got back from India, my mother died suddenly in her sleep but not before she had read my journal of self-discovery. I flew over for the funeral. Aunt Pamela, brave but shaken, always the stoic, recounted their evenings of reading from it.

"You know, Chloe, your mother was so delighted you finally found your wings and took to the sky." She handed me a letter and a scrapbook. "This is for you. She always wanted you to have it".

Page after page of newspaper cuttings and pictures of the beautiful young pianist. As I open the envelope of the letter, a photograph falls to the floor of a handsome and rugged looking man.

Dear Chloe,

When you open this I will be gone. You asked me in the teashop in Lincoln why I gave up my career. I was twenty when I fell deeply in love with Kim, a married man who was both unable and, as it turned out, unwilling to leave his marriage. The man you always knew as your father had always loved me, always been there in the background of my life. With my young broken heart I clung to him and, leaving music behind, quickly became his wife, soon to become a mother and supporter of an ambitious man's career.

Six years on, Kim and I bumped into each other again and spiralled into a passionate love affair. As if the tide took us up, unable to stop ourselves. (Haven't I heard that somewhere before?) You are the product of that union. Kim Slazenger, your birth father, was a well known climber. Killed by an avalanche six months before your birth. The man you have always called father truly loved you and me, both, but was so afraid we might take flight and leave him. He was a good man, Chloe, he saw me through my grief and never threw it back at me. He forgave me, you see, but he always knew he was second best. Not easy to live with that. I promised not to tell you while he was alive and then I lacked the courage. Didn't want to spoil the precious time you and I had together.

When I look at you all I see is Kim. Same constantly enquiring mind, same energy and directness and the same laugh – quick to arrive and so infectious. Same courage to explore and experience. Push the boundaries. You have always been that constant, cherished reminder born of a great love affair. Life is never easy; we all make mistakes and what seem like wrong decisions. Looking back, I know now I should have told you long ago. I am so sorry. Can you forgive me? Talk to Aunt Pamela. She knew Kim too. You have always been so much loved. You do know that, don't you?

Pamela hands me a drink, two thirds gin and little tonic, and the two of us sit in complete silence. The tears come, a great gushing cleansing, like a weight rolling off me and she puts her arms around me and holds me tight. A real bear hug. A tweed coat hug. Very late that night she hands me another envelope full of articles about Kim and his climbing adventures. It is early morning before I put the last piece of paper down, catching sight of the two wooden sabots beside my bed as I do so. Yet another piece of life's jigsaw puzzle. No, Baba is never far away. I locate him inside of myself and his warmth comes as I fall asleep, his hand in mine. "Little Neerja. How you are journeying. Keep swimming. Keep going."

Aunt Pamela and I get really close and when I am not deluging her with questions about Kim, their love affair ("But how did they meet? What did he really look like? How tall was he? What mountains did he climb?), we chatter away comfortably on any subject. (Well, not *any* subject. Not about deep eyes and tumbling black hair.) Pamela gives me hours of her attention, only interrupted by Mrs Plover and yet another cup of tea. My mother's great love affair capturing my romantic imagination. Her devastating loss striking a deep chord within me. I find compassion, too, for the man who was always second best, who brought me up, wanted what he thought was right for me. "She left him, you know, to be with Kim but when Kim died he just held out his arms and took her back in. For the second time. He never looked at another woman. She was always the only one for him." How much he must have loved her. I guess being any kind of best would do just to be with the woman he had adored since a teenager. "His fear of losing you both made him so controlling. You probably know that better than most people, Chloe." My aunt's understatement is said with a wry smile. At last I am getting to know the characters in this play so far. So relieved to understand why I never felt I fitted. Right part, wrong play? Wrong part, right play? But was it? "All is as it is. That is where the challenge lies. The opportunity." The wise words of the beautiful old man. Shame, though, we had to wait till death for honesty and truth to reveal themselves.

Well, I came back to New York, sold the house and Rosie and I have taken up residence in a small apartment in Soho. Rosie leaves soon on a working trip to Peru. She is in love with Chris, a botanist. They too are caught up in that tide of rapture. That current so fierce that there's no resisting. I am so glad to know my mother had that. So excited to have been born from such fierce passion.

Jim has visited twice. An easy uncomplicated sort of guy and now a good friend. I heard, too, from a friend of Sean's who enclosed his airfare and a brief embarrassed note from Sean himself. "Sorry, Chloe. I enjoyed the time we spent together."

But it's the Crab Man, Baba, who is the one constant feature of my life. Me in him. Him in me. Me always inside of myself. Always appearing when I call him. Reminding me to always be myself. Other plains are where I meet him.

Those other plains. That place where beauty hides. Behind those dense human veils, she waits. That love in another. That love for yourself. Just waiting. Waiting to be found. Beyond all outward appearances. (Now, who said that?)

As for me... I spend one day a week down at the 'Ever Open Door' drop-out centre. Each time I look into those rheumy eyes, smell that pungent body odour and breathe that alcohol breath, I remember Dolores and the small stick-thin child that I was, as I squatted beside her on the sidewalk. Right now, though, it's time for more journeying. I am reading *Anna Karenina* for the second time. My imagination is fired and raring to go. The atlas is in my case, the wooden sabots ready to travel with me. Love is in my heart. "Now let me see…where *exactly* is Russia?"

"*Namaste. Om shanti.* Peace."

All my life I have searched for your face.
Today I have found it.

Rumi

About the Author

"Like the heroine of The Crab Man I decided in middle age to make a dramatic change in my life. For the next ten years I felt as if I was on an express train hurtling across countries, continents and through one extraordinary experience after another with little time to take a breath. Love, grief, pain and loss, danger, near-death experiences plus deeply spiritual happenings... one after the other. Life took me to the very edge and back. Living in different communities learning about different traditions and cultures.

"Although this is a novel I really did meet The Crab Man in India and he lives within me always. How? Why? I really don't know, but I know that something happened that brought me peace of mind. I believe that our spirit kicks in to help us when we are lost, down or confused; a force that appears just when we need someone. Some call it a guardian angel - just when we thought all was lost and we are about to sink below the surface, they are there to hold out a hand and pull us back up again. Then they are gone. From the American Indian culture I have learnt to read the signs of nature and draw strength and knowledge from them. They have much to tell us. For the moment I live on a mountainside in a place of great magic where I watch the deep red sun rise over Africa, catch the tiny flickering light of a passing boat on the distant sea and where I count the stars at night. If I was asked to make a suggestion to anyone it would be to "explore who you really are and why you are here."

Claire Wilkinson is the founder of the *Help Our Women Charity* and Logistics Director of the *United World Youth Council*.

The latter charity is an interactive hands-on peace programme designed to foster mutual understanding between young people from countries such as Iraq, Israel, Palestinian Territories, Bosnia etc bringing them together with students who have little or no experience of what it is to live with bombs and/or suppression.

The *Help our Women Charity* has been helping women living under oppression in countries such as Latvia, and is now actively engaged in talks with an organisation in Afghanistan. The goal is to create small groups of English and Irish women sponsoring Afghan women who seek education but have not the means or opportunities.

"Already we are sponsoring two young women in Afghanistan to gain an education. In the future, we will be selling locally-made shawls, jewellery and handcrafts, adhering to Fairtrade principles. Please support their local community by visiting www..helpourwomen.org to find when and where you can buy these goods."

Claire Wilkinson

www.helpourwomen.org

If you would like to participate, make a donation or sponsor the charity, please contact Claire Wilkinson on email: clairewilkins80@hotmail.com

Part of the proceeds of this book will go to supporting young women in Afghanistan who wish to have an education but have neither the means nor support to do so.